AF429106

MURDER IN VITRO

PAULA BERNSTEIN

M&Z PRESS

Murder In Vitro
Copyright © 2017 Paula Bernstein

Third Edition

Cover Design by Kristin Bryant at Kristin Design

M&Z Press Publication Date: May 2024

All Rights Are Reserved.

This is a work of fiction. Names, characters, places, brands, media, and incidents are either the product of the author's imagination or are used fictitiously. Any resemblance to persons, living or dead, actual events, locales or organizations is entirely coincidental.

The author acknowledges the trademarked status and trademark owners of various products referenced in this work of fiction, which have been used without permission. The publication/use of these trademarks is not authorized, associated with, or sponsored by the trademark owners.

Without limiting the rights under copyright reserved above, no part of this book may be used or reproduced without written permission, except in the case of brief quotations embodied in critical articles and reviews.

PRAISE FOR PAULA BERNSTEIN

"Bernstein has written a smart, compelling mystery set in the fascinating world of fertility medicine. With so many believable suspects, In Vitro will keep you guessing right to the end."

MARY MARKS, BESTSELLING AUTHOR OF
THE QUILTING MYSTERY SERIES.

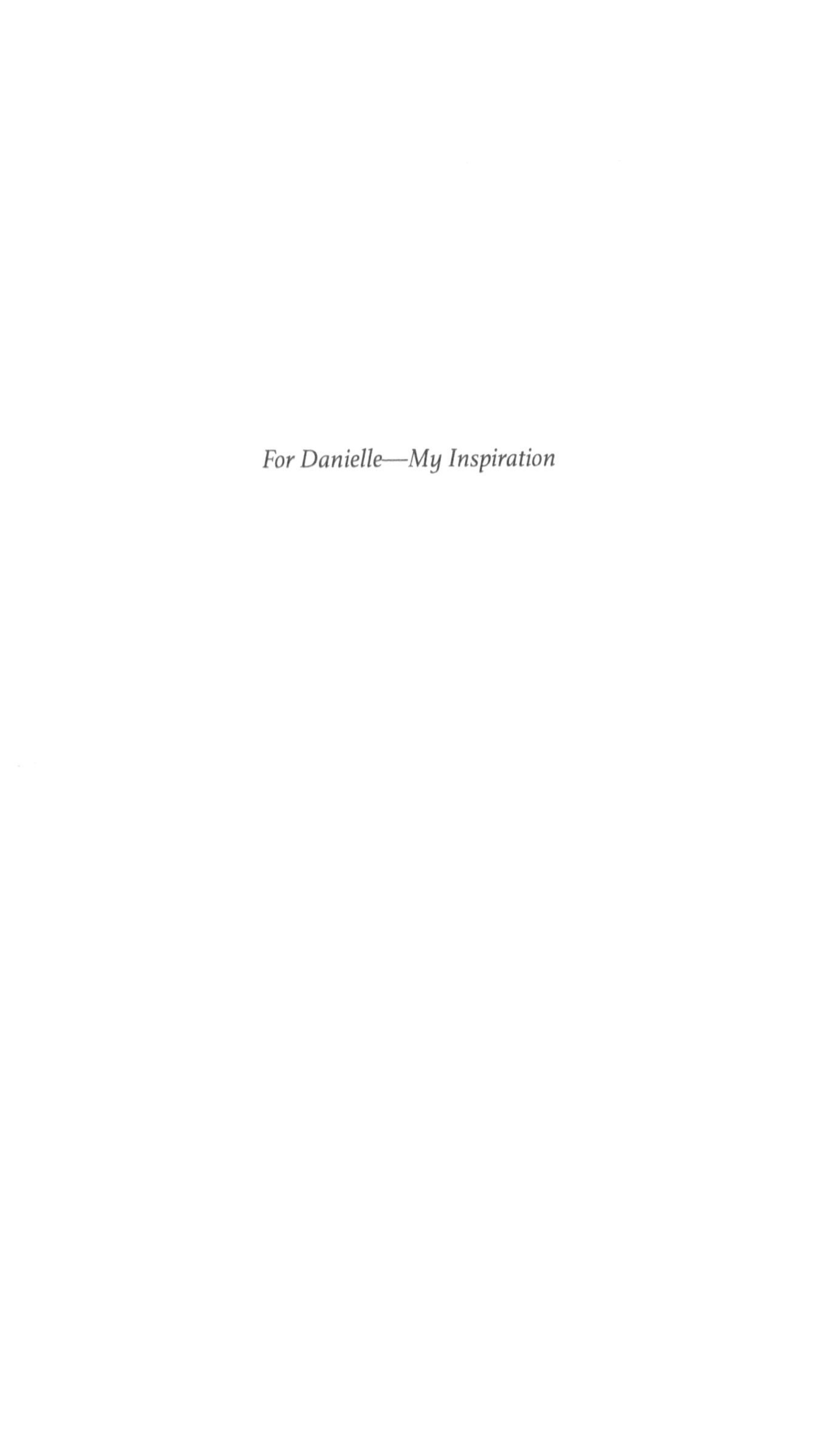

For Danielle—My Inspiration

On July 25, 1978, doctors Patrick Steptoe, Robert Edwards and Jean Purdy, in Manchester, England, electrified the world by announcing the birth of Louise Brown, the first "test tube baby." Louise had been conceived by a fertilization process that took place in the laboratory, after which the embryo was implanted into her mother's uterus. In December of 1981, the first American in vitro baby, Elizabeth Carr, was born.

In the subsequent forty years, despite suspicion and religious objections, the new fertility technology exploded and millions of babies were born to couples who had tried and failed for years to become pregnant. The procedure was particularly helpful for women whose fallopian tubes were blocked.

Over the years the technology became more sophisticated. Genetic testing could be done on just one cell of an embryo to avoid implanting embryos with chromosome defects or known genetic disease. A single sperm could be individually injected into an egg to facilitate conception for couples with very low sperm counts. Women who had previously undergone hysterectomies could create embryos with their own eggs, to be carried by surrogates, and younger women could donate their eggs to others who were not ovulating. Even post-menopausal women could use the technology to have babies.

Although technological innovation proceeded at a rapid pace, society and governments lagged behind in dealing with the complex ethical and legal issues posed by these procedures. Professional societies, such as the ASRM (American Society of Reproductive Medicine), have stepped in to provide some medical guidelines, but legislative and legal guides are lacking and vary by state.

As a gynecologist and obstetrician, I've followed the technology and the ethical issues with great interest and wanted to share some of the fascinating aspects of this medical world with my readers.

IT WAS DARK WHEN THE WOMAN LEFT the rundown storefront in the mini-mall. A streetlight was out just opposite the mall parking lot, and the sky was overcast. All this made her uneasy.

She hadn't parked in the lot, not wanting to risk any of the others seeing her car, and perhaps making note of the license plate. Instead, she had parked around the corner, on a quiet residential street.

She wasn't ordinarily a fearful person but she found herself feeling anxious. Picking up her pace, she took the car key out of her purse and stole a quick look over her shoulder. Every time she went to one of these meetings, she swore it would be the last, but she kept on going. The work was so important.

Breathing a sigh of relief, she spotted the white car, pointed the remote toward it, and unlocked the door. Then, obeying the tense feeling in the pit of her stomach, she ran for it.

I WINCED AS THE ANESTHESIOLOGIST shoved an 18-gauge needle into my wrist vein, and deftly attached the IV fluid without spilling a drop of blood onto the clean, white sheets.

"Are you okay, Dr. Kline?" the young doctor asked.

I gave him a reassuring smile. It wasn't his fault I hated being a patient. The gurney was cold, the pillow was hard, and I felt far too vulnerable wearing that absurd hospital gown. I should have been the one in scrubs, wielding the knife. Not to mention the irony of being a successful obstetrician and not being able to get pregnant on my own.

"I'm fine," I said. "Are we ready to go in?"

"As soon as Dr. Waldman arrives."

Louise Waldman was my friend and colleague, and the senior partner in Westside Fertility Associates, the best reproductive technology practice in Los Angeles. I was about to undergo an egg retrieval, the next step in my in vitro fertilization procedure.

My fiancé, LAPD Detective Daniel Ross, had driven me to the surgery center that morning and had gone into another room to do his part, collecting a sperm specimen to fertilize all those eggs. I was the first case, scheduled for 7:30 a.m.

"Hi, love." Daniel came into the pre-op room, escorted by one of the OR nurses. "Mission accomplished. Are you ready?"

"I'm good to go. Just waiting for Louise to get here."

Daniel looked at his watch. "It's seven forty-five. Is she usually late?"

"She's usually half an hour early," the nurse said. "Let me check with the front desk and see if she called. Maybe she got stuck in traffic."

It was fifteen minutes before the nurse returned and I was beginning to worry.

"Did you reach her?" I asked.

"No. We tried her home number and her cell. There's no answer."

"Have you tried calling her husband, Hank? He'd probably know what time she left the house."

"We tried his office but it isn't open yet. We left a voicemail asking him to phone as soon as he gets in."

Daniel checked the traffic on his cell phone. "It's all green," he said, "and no report of any traffic accident between here and the Westside."

"I'm really sorry, Dr. Kline. I'll ask Dr. Tanaka to do your egg retrieval. I'm sure she'd be happy to do it."

Dr. Nori Tanaka was the newest and youngest doctor in the practice. She'd been an endocrine fellow at Memorial Hospital and I liked her a lot. I had no issue with her doing my egg retrieval but I had an uneasy feeling in the pit of my stomach. It was totally out of character for Louise not to show up for my procedure.

"Daniel, if she isn't here, and doesn't call in fifteen

minutes, do you think we should have the police check her house? Or am I being paranoid?"

"I think you're being appropriately worried. If she doesn't show up, I'll call the station and have someone go to her home. She could be sick, or maybe she fell and broke a leg, and can't get to a phone."

Daniel didn't mention the worst possibility but he didn't have to. We both knew what it was.

Nori Tanaka came in to talk to me, and at 8:15 a.m., they wheeled me into the operating room.

Daniel squeezed my hand as I left. "Don't worry, sweetheart. I've got this."

CHAPTER TWO

D ANIEL WAS CONCERNED AND SO WAS the staff at Westside Fertility.

"Louise is the most responsible physician I know," Nori Tanaka said. "Nothing like this has ever happened before. If she was delayed, she would have notified us. It doesn't make sense for her not to show up for Hannah."

Daniel agreed. Louise and Hannah weren't close personal friends but they had a long-standing professional relationship. He called the West Los Angeles Station and arranged for someone check Louise's house. The circumstance of a doctor being late for a surgery and unreachable might not ordinarily have set off alarm bells, but Daniel Ross was a detective whose instincts were taken seriously by his colleagues. A patrol car was sent immediately.

At 9:00 a.m., Hank Waldman's office returned Daniel's call. Hank, Louise's husband, was on a flight back to Los Angeles from a New York business trip, and couldn't be reached until his plane landed at 12:34 p.m. The office had ordered a limousine to pick him up and take him home. He wasn't expected back at work until Monday morning. Daniel thanked Hank's secretary, declined to leave a message, and said he would call Hank later that day, at home.

It hadn't taken long for the police to do a house check.

"She's not there, Detective Ross," the patrolman said. "There's a BMW and a Mercedes in the garage. The alarm is set and there's no evidence of a break-in. We called her security company and got into the house through a window. No sign of any disturbance. The bed is made, the kitchen is clean. There's no indication that she'd had breakfast or made coffee, or even slept at home, and there's no obvious trace of violence."

"Thanks, guys," Daniel said. "I appreciate the fast response."

So where was she and why hadn't she shown up for Hannah?

CHAPTER THREE

W HEN HANNAH'S PROCEDURE WAS over, she was transferred to the post-operative suite.

Dr. Tanaka came out of the operating room and found Daniel.

"Everything went smoothly," she said. "You can go in as soon as she wakes up. Any news about Louise?"

Daniel filled her in.

"Detective Ross, do you think I should report Dr. Waldman as missing? No doctor in this practice has ever failed to show up for a scheduled procedure. I can't help feeling that something's very wrong."

"Then you should file a report with missing persons. I know the detective who heads that department. I can speak to her and offer my help. I took the day off, so I'm available to start an investigation. Which I can do, as soon as I've seen Hannah."

I woke up from anesthesia with a fuzzy brain and really bad cramps. I thought about saying something, or moving my hand, but somehow, the signal didn't make it from my brain to my body. When I managed to open my eyes, Nori Tanaka was smiling at me.

"All done," she said. "Everything went smoothly. Do you need anything for pain?"

"Pretty crampy," I managed to say.

She told the nurse to give me a dose of IV morphine.

"You'll be able to go home in about an hour," Nori said.

I could feel the cramps starting to subside. "Louise?" I asked.

"We haven't heard from her."

"Can I see Daniel?"

"I'll have one of the nurses bring him in."

I must have dozed off, because Daniel was sitting beside my bed when I opened my eyes.

He took my hand. "They're making our embryos as we speak."

"That's great. How many?"

"You laid a dozen eggs."

I laughed, and then my happiness subsided. "What did you find out about Louise? Did they check her house?"

I was dreading his answer.

"She isn't there, Hannah. There's no trace of violence, but she must have come home at some point because her car is there."

"What did her husband say?"

"He's on a plane from New York and can't be reached. As soon as he lands and gets home, I'm planning to go see him."

"So, where is she?" I demanded.

"I don't know, Hannah. She's missing."

As soon as Nori Tanaka had called the police to report Louise Waldman missing, Daniel phoned the head of the division, Detective Tess Duncan.

"Hey, Daniel."

"Hi, Tess. I'm calling about a missing persons report that just got called in on Louise Waldman. She's Hannah's doctor, and she failed to show up this morning for a surgical procedure. I sent a car to her house, but no one was home. I'd like to offer my help. I'm at the surgery center adjacent to her office, so I can talk to her staff and colleagues."

"Does she live alone?" Tess asked.

"She's married and has a son, but her husband has been in New York on business this week and the son is away at college. The husband is due home later today. I'd like to talk to him as well."

"Are you sure you aren't jumping the gun? Maybe she got drunk last night and is sleeping it off in a hotel room, or maybe she ran off with a lover."

"Anything is possible," Daniel acknowledged. "But not showing up for a procedure on a colleague, who has referred a large number of patients, is professional suicide. We are talking about one of the most highly respected physicians in town."

"Okay. I trust your judgment. I'm happy to have your help. You know how understaffed my department is. You'd better clear your participation with the Captain so neither of us gets in trouble. Make sure you keep me in the loop. In the meantime, I'll prioritize this case and assign someone to take the lead."

"Thanks, Tess. I'll call you later and let you know what I've learned," Daniel said.

Daniel turned to Dr. Tanaka. "Did Dr. Waldman keep a calendar?"

"We all do," she answered.

"Let's look at her office."

Louise's office reflected what Hannah had told Daniel about the doctor's style. It was comfortable and unpretentious. The desk was piled with papers, surrounding a computer terminal, and there was a large bookcase on one wall, haphazardly stocked with medical books and journals.

When Daniel seated himself at the desk, Dr. Tanaka quickly collected all the papers and put them in one pile.

"You can't look at these," she said. "They're confidential patient laboratory results."

"Relax," Daniel said. "I'm not trying to violate patient privacy."

He opened the desk drawers, most of which contained office supplies, and finally found a leather-bound weekly diary. Nori Tanaka looked over his shoulder, as if she were afraid he would steal something valuable.

"I haven't seen one of these in a long time," he said.

Daniel settled himself in the chair and opened the diary. It was sparsely populated with theater and concert dates, and occasional midweek lunch appointments. The current week was almost blank, except for a notation on Thursday at 7:30 p.m., *FPA*.

"Do you know what these initials stand for?" Daniel asked, glancing up at Dr. Tanaka.

"Not a clue," she said.

Daniel flipped backwards through the pages and found several more FPA notations, all on Thursday nights.

"I'm going to take this with me as evidence. I need to review it more closely. I'll give you a receipt. I'd also like a printout of Dr. Waldman's professional schedule for the past three months."

"I'll tell the front desk. We'll have to delete all the patient appointments." Dr. Tanaka reached for the phone and activated the intercom.

When she was done, Daniel said, "I'd like to ask you a few questions. When did you last see Dr. Waldman?"

"Yesterday afternoon, around five-thirty. I was leaving. Louise was in her office doing paperwork. I waved goodbye on my way out."

"Had she mentioned anything to you about her plans for the evening?"

"No."

"Did she seem upset or preoccupied over the past few days or weeks? Any change in her behavior?"

"I'm sorry. I honestly didn't notice anything unusual."

"Do you remember what she was wearing yesterday?"

"I do. Louise wore the same kind of clothes every day: slacks, black, gray or navy; and a long-sleeved, tailored blouse, usually white, beige, or occasionally a pastel. I think she was wearing navy slacks, a white blouse, and a red and navy scarf."

"Thanks," Daniel said. "Can you introduce me to the other two doctors in your practice?"

"They're both at our satellite office in the Valley today," she said. "But I'll introduce you to the rest of our staff. You should have time to talk to them before Hannah is ready to leave."

CHAPTER FIVE

I'D BEEN DRIFTING IN AND OUT OF sleep, in a comfortable, morphine-induced haze. The cramps were gone, and when I finally felt alert enough to open my eyes, the clock said 10:45 a.m. I looked around, hoping that Louise would be in post-op with me. She wasn't.

"Are you ready to try to get up?" a nurse asked.

"I think so. When can I go home?"

"As soon as you're up and dressed," she said. "I'll bring your clothes and help you to the bathroom."

"Can you tell Daniel I'm almost ready to leave?" I asked.

"Of course." The nurse took out my IV.

I pushed myself into an upright position and allowed her to help me off the gurney. When I got back from the bathroom, Daniel was waiting.

"Hi, Any news?"

"Afraid not. I'm officially helping the missing persons division, and I've interviewed the staff, but no one seems to know anything useful. If you're not too tired, on the way out, I thought I'd see if I could review the security tapes from the garage."

"I'm not tired. I've been sleeping all morning and I feel fine. Let's do it," I said.

We took the elevator down to the garage level. Daniel had parked his Mustang close by.

"Why don't I get you comfortable in the passenger seat, and then I'll go flash my LAPD credentials at the parking attendant."

"Not a chance. I'm coming with you. You can pretend I'm your partner, Brenda."

Daniel gave me a skeptical look, but clearly decided it wasn't worth arguing.

The attendant was adequately intimidated by Daniel's badge and happy to cooperate.

He escorted us to a lower level which was reserved for tenants and their employees, and pointed to Louise's space, near the elevator. Daniel and I looked for security cameras and were pleased to note that the garage seemed adequately covered.

"I'd like to see yesterday afternoon's footage, from five o'clock on, from the cameras near Dr. Waldman's car and at the lot exit," Daniel said.

We were taken back to the parking office, and introduced to a security guard who was watching the camera feeds. Daniel flashed his badge again and made his request.

"Is something wrong?" the guard asked.

"Dr. Waldman is missing. She was last seen in her office at about five-thirty yesterday afternoon. I'd like to see if and when she left the building."

"Pull up a chair," the guard said.

Daniel insisted I take it, while he looked over the guard's shoulder. The film was backtracked to the requested time and we fast-forwarded the camera feed near Louise's car. At

5:55 p.m., a woman opened the door of the BMW and seated herself in the driver's seat.

"Is that her?" Daniel asked.

"Definitely," I said.

We watched the feed as she backed out of her spot and drove out of range of the camera. We continued watching to see if any car was following. The lot was almost empty and we saw no one.

We switched to the camera at the exit and watched the BMW leave the building. No other car left for the next half hour.

"Thank you," Daniel said. He handed an empty flash drive to the guard. "I'd like a copy of that data, just in case."

We returned to Daniel's car and drove home.

"How about I make you something to eat?" Daniel asked, as we pulled into the garage. "You must be famished."

"I am. What's our plan for the rest of the afternoon?"

"Your plan is to sit, while I fix some coffee and an omelet for you," he said. "Louise's husband should be home by one-thirty. I'm going over there to break the news, and to see if he knows anything helpful."

"Can I come with you?"

Daniel gave me a look. "You know you can't, Hannah."

"You can't blame a girl for trying," I said. "I'm really worried."

"I know you are. If you want to help, I have a job for you. I have Louise's personal calendar, as well as a printout of her office calendar for the past three months. Could you review them both, and see if you can make sense out of some of the abbreviations? They might have medical meaning to you that I don't recognize."

"Sounds like a good division of labor," I said. "I'll get on it as soon as I've had my caffeine. You will keep me posted, won't you?"

"I'll call you as soon as I learn anything new," he promised.

Daniel removed some eggs, butter and cheddar cheese from the refrigerator, and started a pot of coffee. I sat back and watched him take care of me, reminding myself of how lucky I was to find such a wonderful guy, after the death of my husband Ben. Just as soon as I became pregnant, we could start planning our wedding. I recognized that most people thought I had things in the wrong order, but unlike my ovaries, our wedding wasn't racing my biological clock.

Daniel handed me a large mug of coffee. I took that first special sip and sighed with contentment. If it weren't for the mystery of Louise, everything in my life would be perfect.

CHAPTER SIX

T HE WALDMANS LIVED IN A CHARMING, gray Cape Cod home in Pacific Palisades. Daniel parked his car in front of the white picket gate, walked up to the front door, and rang the doorbell.

The door was opened by Hank Waldman, a tall, slightly overweight man in his sixties. He had thick, salt-and-pepper hair, and was wearing a pair of gold-rimmed bifocal glasses, and an old pair of sweats, and sneakers.

Daniel held out his LAPD identification. "Detective Daniel Ross, Mr. Waldman. May I come in?"

"What's this about?" Hank asked. "Has something happened to Louise?"

"We don't know," Daniel said. "She seems to be missing."

"How can she possibly be missing?" Hank opened the door wider and gestured for Daniel to follow.

He led Daniel through the formal front of the house and back to a comfortable, somewhat untidy den, scattered with newspapers and books. A briefcase lay open on a large walnut desk.

Hank began to pace back and forth from the door to the windows, running his hands through his formerly tidy hair.

"When was the last time you heard from her?" Daniel asked.

"I spoke to her Wednesday night. It was a perfectly ordinary conversation. "

"Did she say anything about her plans for the next day?"

Hank shook his head. "What do you mean she's missing?"

"Louise failed to show up this morning for a surgical procedure, something that's completely out of character. Her office couldn't reach her, either at home or on her cell."

"Did anyone come and check the house?"

"We sent a police cruiser and they called your security company. She must have come home from the office yesterday, because they reported that her car was in the garage and there was no sign of a break-in or violence. Her calendar said she had an FPA appointment at seven-thirty last night. Does that mean anything to you?"

"No," Hank said. "Have you checked the hospitals? What if she got sick in the middle of the night and called 911?"

"Of course, we checked the hospitals and the 911 records. That's standard procedure. We haven't been able to locate her. Is it possible that she went somewhere in your car instead of hers?"

"Come with me," Hank said. "I haven't been in the garage since I got home. A limo dropped me off."

The two of them proceeded through a pristine kitchen to the inner garage door. Daniel noted that there were no dishes in the dishwasher or in the sink. It appeared that no one had eaten dinner or breakfast. The garage had room for three cars and was extremely orderly, with tools, two bicycles and camping equipment hanging from hooks along the wall. Louise's black BMW was in the middle space, next to a large, gray Mercedes sedan.

"That's my car," Hank said. "It looks like she may have taken the Honda, our son George's car. It's not here."

"Why would she take his car?"

"I think she feels a little uncomfortable in the new BMW. She worries that it's too conspicuous."

"Where is your son, Mr. Waldman?" Daniel asked.

"George is at Dartmouth. He doesn't need his car there."

"Give me the license number and color of the car," Daniel said. "I'll put out a BOLO on it. If you don't mind, I'd like to look at the master bedroom and her study."

The bedroom was neat, except for a red and navy silk scarf draped over a chair. Daniel fingered it. It matched the scarf described by Nori Tanaka.

"It looks as if your wife may have come home and changed clothes. She wore this scarf to the office."

Hank opened a large, well organized closet. "There's the hamper where she puts clothes to go to the cleaners," he said.

The outfit was there. Daniel checked the pockets, which were empty.

"Any chance you could figure out what she changed into?"

"I have no idea. Does it matter? For God's sake, do something constructive."

"Knowing what she was wearing might help with a description. What about her purse? Is it here? She was carrying a navy blue one," Daniel said.

Hank glanced at a row of cubbyholes with purses in assorted colors. "I don't see it."

"Cell phone?"

"We could try her iPad," Hank said. "She's got Find My Phone on it."

Hank opened a door into a small study with a built-in desk and bookshelves. The iPad was beside a laptop, he booted it up and handed it to Daniel.

"Found it," Daniel said. "Looks like it's on a street just off Pico, in the Mid-Wilshire district. I'm going to head there now and have a patrol car meet me. I'll need to take the iPad with me as evidence Can you give me the code?"

Hank scribbled something on a scrap of paper and handed it to Daniel.

"Do you have any photos of Louise I could borrow?"

There were a number of family photos scattered around the study, and hung on the master bedroom walls. Hank took down a recent head shot of his wife, wearing a white physician's coat.

"Do you have a color copier, by any chance?" Daniel asked.

"In my office." Hank walked back to the den, printed out several copies, and handed them to Daniel.

"Thanks, that's helpful."

Hank reached out, digging his fingers tightly into Daniel's upper arms. "Detective, please call me as soon as you know anything."

"Of course, I will," Daniel said.

CHAPTER SEVEN

A FTER DANIEL LEFT, I MADE MYSELF more coffee, supplemented it with a few chocolate chip cookies, and took my snack and Louise's calendar into my study. We had just moved into our beautiful new home, and being there soothed me. My office had a gorgeous view of the canyon. It seemed impossible that something could be so wrong on such a beautiful day.

I created a new file for Louise on my computer, and made a list of dates, names and abbreviations that her calendar contained for the three months prior to her disappearance. I cross-checked my list with the printout from her office. The desk calendar was primarily personal. The office calendar noted professional meetings. Most of the entries were straightforward.

There were two notations that said "PPLA Board." I suspected that stood for Planned Parenthood of Los Angeles. I knew that Louise had been an active supporter. I reached into my desk drawer and pulled out a recent invitation to a fundraiser. Louise was listed as one of the sponsors. I knew Frances Conners, the medical director of Planned

Parenthood. I was planning to attend that fundraiser next week, and I would try to have a word with her.

The notation FPA was a cipher. I couldn't find any reference to it on the internet, but it was apparently a monthly meeting that Louise had been attending. I put it in bold on my list.

Most of the names on her personal calendar were female and first names only. I assumed they were friends and figured that Hank, or Louise's secretary, would know who they were. There was also a lunch meeting with a Roger Alexander. I googled him and came up with a medical malpractice attorney. That was interesting.

I went to the Medical Board of California website and checked Louise's name. There was no record of any malpractice settlements. It was difficult to practice medicine these days without someone suing you for a less than perfect outcome.

Since the Board only listed closed cases, I moved on to the website of the Los Angeles Superior Court and looked for any suits filed against Louise, personally, or the practice. There was one, and it was recent: Bachman vs. Waldman and Westside Fertility Associates. I'd have to find out what that was about.

I put the calendars safely away in a drawer. Enough detecting for the day. I selected a new novel, curled up in my armchair with an afghan on my lap, and treated myself to a well- earned rest as I anxiously awaited word from Daniel.

CHAPTER EIGHT

D ANIEL CALLED TESS DUNCAN IN Missing Persons and updated her on his activities.

"I'm heading over to Mid-Wilshire to see if I can track down Louise's phone. Can you send a couple of your people to meet me, or should I phone my partner?"

"Sounds like you've been busy," Tess said. "I've assigned Jason Cole to take the lead in this case. I'll have him meet you there."

"Thanks," Daniel said. "I'll keep you posted."

Damn it. Daniel knew Cole by reputation as young, aggressive, narrow-minded, and likely to spend more time defending his territory than working the case. No doubt he'd go out of his way to demonstrate that he was the Alpha Male. Daniel would have to be tactful. Daniel sighed. He would have much preferred working this case with his partner, Detective Brenda Jordan.

The iPad app led him to a side street, west of La Cienega and south of Pico. Pico Boulevard was a downscale shopping area, full of older, one-story shops. The side streets were modest residential ones with small, older homes, occasional

Spanish duplexes, and neat front lawns. Daniel drove past a café, a used furniture store, and a mini-mall. He turned a corner, following the iPad's GPS and spotted a silver Honda.

Daniel pulled up behind it and checked the plates. It was definitely George Waldman's car. He opened his door, put on a pair of latex gloves, and circled the car slowly, peering inside the windows. Daniel tried the door and was surprised to find it unlocked. It was remarkable that the car hadn't been stolen.

He returned to his car, opened the trunk and removed some plastic evidence bags. He photographed the Honda's interior and began searching for the cell phone. He finally found it, on the floor, underneath the passenger seat. It was almost out of battery. Next to it, was the Honda's key. He photographed both items and put them in separate bags.

He checked the glove compartment, which was empty except for registration and insurance information. The driver's side pocket contained a small umbrella and a packet of tissues. The only other item in the car was an Aqua Fina water bottle, in the cup holder between the seats. He put all the remaining items in bags and labeled them.

Daniel opened the trunk by pressing the remote on the car key through the plastic bag. He held his breath, fearing the trunk might contain Louise's decomposing body, and was relieved to discover nothing more than old gym towels and dirty sneakers.

As he was sorting through the contents of the trunk, a patrol car with two policemen pulled up and two officers got out.

"You Daniel Ross?" one of them asked. He was tall and wiry, with dark, curly hair, slicked back with gel, and a fashionable five o'clock shadow.

"I am. Jason Cole?" Daniel offered a hand.

Cole shook it. "What did you find?"

"Nothing good," Daniel said. "This is her son's car. Her husband said she must have driven it last night because hers is in their garage. Her phone and the car key were on the floor, on the passenger side. Since women don't usually leave their cars unlocked, with their phones and keys on the floor, I have to assume she disappeared just as she got to her car. I've photographed everything and put the car's contents in evidence bags."

"What's on the phone?" Cole asked.

"It's almost out of battery," Daniel said. "I thought we should take it to the station, have it dusted for prints, plug it in, and check it there."

Cole turned to the other cop. "Start canvassing the homes closest to the car. See if anyone saw or heard anything unusual."

"You check along Pico," he ordered Daniel. "See if we can figure out where she went last night."

Daniel gritted his teeth. He resented taking orders from a subordinate, but it was Cole's case. This wasn't the time to pull rank.

"You should probably call the evidence guys and get the car towed in so we can have them go over it," Daniel said.

"Yeah, I'm calling. I'll wait here for them."

Daniel pulled out the photos he had of Louise and passed them out.

"These should help with canvassing," he said.

He walked to the corner and turned left. The mini-mall contained a discount furniture store, a falafel place, a Pay Day Loan office, and a dry cleaners. Daniel showed his credentials and Louise's photo, and drew a blank. There was also an empty storefront with a "For Lease" sign and a phone number. Cheap shades hid the interior. Daniel was copying the phone number when his cell rang. It was Brenda.

"Where are you?" she asked.

"On Pico, a few blocks west of La Cienega, why?"

"Good, you're close by. We got a call about a woman's body, found in a construction site dumpster off Cadillac, just north of the 10 Freeway. Can you meet me there? I hope it's not your missing doctor."

Daniel felt a sudden spasm in the pit of his stomach. He hoped the body wasn't Louise's either, but his gut was telling him otherwise.

CHAPTER NINE

WHEN DANIEL ARRIVED, HE SAW THE coroner's van, the crime scene technicians, and four patrol cars. His partner, Detective Brenda Jordan, was in conversation with Dr. Bill Pincus, one of the County medical examiners. The dumpster was at the end of the street closest to the freeway, and next to a house that had been torn down to the studs and was being renovated. A police photographer was on a ladder, taking pictures of the dumpster's contents. There was a black plastic tarp on the ground.

Daniel put on gloves and shoe covers, greeted the patrol team, and joined Brenda.

"Hi," she said. "Why don't you climb up and take a look. See if this body could be your missing doctor?"

Daniel took a deep breath, waited for the photographer to finish, climbed to the top of the ladder and looked down. The body was clearly that of a woman. She was sprawled on her stomach, legs splayed out, lying at an angle, with her head partly concealed by debris. She was wearing jeans, a long-sleeved, black T-shirt, and black trainers. What could be seen of her hair was gray.

"Are we ready to remove her from the dumpster?" Daniel asked. "I can't really tell anything from up here."

Brenda motioned to two guys wearing hazmat suits. They picked up the tarp, set up a second ladder, and climbed into the dumpster. A few minutes later, the woman's body was on the ground.

Large chunks of her face and neck, and the exposed tissue on her wrists and around her ankles were missing. Rats had been feasting on the dumpster contents. Bill Pincus bent down for a closer look.

"Clearly female. I estimate her age at sixty. She's been dead about twelve hours, judging by the temperature and rigor," Bill said.

"She's the right body type and age to be Louise Waldman," Daniel said. "The hair length and color matches as well, but since we're missing much of her face, we'll obviously need fingerprints, dental records or DNA to make a positive identification. Did the rats destroy the finger tips?"

Bill Pincus bent down and examined the hands. "No. We should be able to get prints."

"Can you tell cause of death?" Daniel asked.

"I don't see any obvious stab or bullet wounds, so we can probably rule out guns and knives. I also don't see any indication of head trauma. I'll need to look more closely at the hyoid bone to see if she was strangled, and do a toxicology screen."

"We found Louise's car, just south of Pico, not far from here. Her cell phone and car key were in it but not her purse. Did you find a navy blue purse in the dumpster by any chance?" Daniel asked.

"That would be a no," said a voice from inside the dumpster. One of the two crime scene techs poked his head above the dumpster's edge. "It's mostly construction debris."

"Who found her?"

"The next door neighbor," Brenda said. "Apparently, the building contractor had finished the demolition and wasn't expecting the next crew to start until Monday. The neighbor was cleaning out his garage and thought he'd take advantage of the dumpster to throw out a few things that were too big for his garbage cans. He climbed up on a ladder, looked over the edge, and saw the body. I suspect that's the last time he uses someone else's dumpster."

"I assume you've assigned a few guys to canvass the block and find out if anyone heard or saw anything suspicious last night," Daniel said.

"You assume correctly," answered Brenda.

Daniel turned to Bill. "Can we get her to the County morgue and get an ID as quickly as possible? I don't want to say anything to her husband until we're sure."

"You know Louise Waldman personally?" Bill asked.

"In a manner of speaking. She was Hannah's doctor. The odds are that this is her body, and I'm not looking forward to breaking the news to my fiancée."

CHAPTER TEN

I T WAS ALMOST DINNER TIME WHEN Daniel finally called. Zoe was home from school. Emilia, our housekeeper, had made some roast chicken, and I was debating whether to wait, or eat without him.

"Hey, Hannah. It's me."

I could tell from his voice that the news wasn't good. I left Zoe in the kitchen and took the phone into the den, so I could talk privately.

"Have you found her?"

"I'm afraid so. She's dead, sweetheart. Her body was found in a dumpster near the 10 Freeway."

"Oh, God." The tears spilled from my eyes and I started to shake. "Not again. Why are people I know and care about getting killed? Am I some kind of murder Typhoid Mary?"

"Of course not. I wish I could come home right now but I've got to break the news to her husband, and have the evidence team go over her house and confiscate her computer. I'm so sorry. I know how much you cared about her."

I disconnected the call and sat there, numb.

"Are you okay, Mommy?" Zoe was standing in the doorway.

"I'm okay, pumpkin. I just got some sad news about a friend."

Zoe climbed into my lap and gave me a big hug. She didn't say anything, just sat there, her warm little body providing comfort and love. Somehow, she always knew the right thing to do. I held her tight for a while, taking deep breaths to calm myself, until I could talk without crying.

"How about some dinner?"

CHAPTER ELEVEN

"Have something to eat," Brenda said to Daniel, as they drove to the Waldman's house.

Brenda could always be relied upon for snack food. She reached under her seat and handed him a plastic bag. In the past, it would have contained doughnuts, but Brenda was watching her weight. There were several pieces of fruit and some string cheese.

Daniel's stomach was still churning from the sight of Louise's body. He hadn't had lunch, and doubted there would be time for dinner, but he had no appetite.

"Thanks," he said. "Maybe later."

"This one is really personal for you, isn't it?"

"Hannah was very upset when I told her. Louise was such a nice woman."

"Someone didn't think so," Brenda said. "We'll find the bastard who did this. I promise."

They pulled up in front of the Waldman's house and rang the doorbell. Hank Waldman answered the door immediately and saw the news on their faces.

"No," he yelled. "It's not true."

"I'm so sorry, Mr. Waldman," Daniel said. "We found her body a few hours ago and identified it positively with fingerprints."

"Who would do this?"

"We're hoping you can help us answer that," Daniel said. "Did Louise have any enemies that you know of? Was there anyone with a reason to hate her?"

Hank motioned them inside. "Louise brought joy to so many people. I can't think of anyone who would have had a reason to kill her. Maybe it was just some psychotic mugger."

"We'll be looking into all the possibilities," Daniel said.

Hank was pacing the floor again, his shoulders shaking, his fists tight. Daniel could see he was fighting for control.

"How did she get along with her partners?" Daniel asked. "Was there any friction that you know about?"

Hank started to shake his head, and then paused to think about his answer.

"Louise was very fond of her youngest associate, Nori Tanaka. Her two senior partners are Ian Price and Kaspar Nazari. The three of them didn't always get along. I think they had different visions for the practice, but I can't imagine that either one of them would have any reason to want Louise dead."

"Would they benefit financially?" Daniel asked.

"I can't answer that," Hank said. "I would have to review the partnership agreement and Louise's will, and at the moment, that is the last thing on my mind."

"I understand. We can talk about some of that later. Mr. Waldman, we're sending an evidence team for your wife's computer and her papers, and to search the house. We're hoping to find some clue to where she may have gone last night, and whether her killing was related to that meeting or was random. We'll try to do our search as quickly as possible."

"When can I bury her?" Hank asked. "I have to call my son, and notify our family and friends."

"As soon as the autopsy is complete, sir. The coroner's office will let you know."

"I still can't believe it," Hank's voice broke, his eyes filled with tears, and he ran his hands over his face and hair, wiping the wet streaks from his cheeks.

"I'm so sorry." Daniel handed Hank one of his cards. "Please call me if you think of anything I should know, or if you need anything."

"I will never get used to this part of the job," Brenda said as they left the house. "At least we know the husband didn't kill her. He was in New York when she died."

"We need to check the flight manifest," Daniel said. "Being in New York doesn't rule out hiring someone to kill your spouse."

"True," Brenda said. "We should get a copy of Louise's will and the partnership agreement. Why don't you head home? I'll take care of the paperwork. Looks like we aren't going to have the weekend off, and I imagine Hannah could use your company right now."

The house was dark when Daniel arrived home. Hannah had left a light on in the entryway for him. He changed into pajamas in the bathroom, and tiptoed quietly into the bedroom, so as not to wake her. He needn't have bothered.

She was sitting up in bed, in the dark, her arms wrapped around her knees, staring out at nothing.

Daniel sat next to her and drew her into his arms. She rested her head on his shoulder and started to cry. He just held her.

"Why would anyone want to kill Louise?"

"I don't know, Hannah, but I'll do my best to find out."

"I want to help, Daniel."

"I know you do," he said. "Did you find anything in the calendars?"

"I've got a list for you, of people she had lunch with. I'm sure you can find out who they are from her phone or from Hank. I couldn't figure out what FPA means, but obviously it's important."

"Anything else?" Daniel asked.

"Louise has a pending malpractice suit. Her lawyer's name is Roger Anderson. Maybe the person who is suing her was angry enough to take it further."

"Good work. I'll put the lawyer and the plaintiff on my interview list."

"One more thing," Hannah said. "Louise was on the board of Planned Parenthood. I don't know if there is any connection to her death, but I do know the medical director in LA fairly well. I could talk to her and see what I can find out."

"You have been busy." Daniel stroked her hair. "Let's sleep on this and see where the investigation leads me. I'll certainly take you up on your offer to talk to the medical director."

Hannah lifted the edge of the quilt so that Daniel could join her. He slipped into bed and cradled her until she fell asleep.

CHAPTER TWELVE

S INCE IT WAS SATURDAY, THE MEETING of the murder team started at 9:00 a.m. instead of 7:30 a.m. Daniel brought bagels and cream cheese, and Brenda started a large pot of coffee. Besides the two of them, the team included Izzy Washington, the department I.T. genius; Jason Cole, on loan from Missing Persons; and three younger detectives from the Homicide division.

While Izzy and Brenda booted up their laptops, Daniel, standing in front of a large cork board on which he had pinned the murder photos, turned to face the team.

He cleared his throat. "Okay. You all know that yesterday the body of Dr. Louise Waldman was found in a dumpster near the 10 Freeway. We found her car, car keys and cell phone on a side street, just south of Pico, not far from the site of the body dump. The car and its contents are currently being analyzed by forensics. Jason, you did some canvassing in the vicinity of the car. What did you find?"

Cole took out his notes and quickly scanned them. "We canvassed all the houses on both sides of the street, but most people weren't home at that hour. I can go back there this morning and try again."

"Thanks," Daniel said. "One of my guys can go with you to help. It's a big job."

"We also checked all the businesses on Pico within a two block radius of the car," Cole continued. "Most of them, except for two fast food places, close at 6 p.m. and no one recognized the photo of Dr. Waldman. We did get all available security footage to review."

"Thanks," Daniel said. "Now, as I see it, we have several lines of investigation. First, as always, is the husband. We've been told he was in New York all week on a business trip and only came home after Louise disappeared. We need to confirm it, and to check his calls to see if there's any evidence this could have been a murder for hire. Along those lines, we need to go where the money is."

"I assume," said Izzy, "that you'd like me to check flight manifests, the Waldman financials, and Dr. Waldman's will."

"Right," Daniel said. "The will and a copy of the partnership agreement for the practice should be in the boxes of files we took from the house last night. Brenda and I will interview all the partners, but before we do, I want to know if they benefit financially from Louise's death.

"Next, we have Louise Waldman's computer, phone and iPad. There was a designation that said FPA at seven-thirty p.m. on her calendar. We haven't been able to figure out what that means. We should scour her emails, web browsing, and Facebook page, if she has one, to see if we can find out where she went that night. I have a list, from her personal calendar, of people she saw in the weeks leading up to her death. We need to identify and talk to each of them."

"That's going to take me awhile," Izzy said.

"It isn't a one person job. Feel free to select the most computer literate detectives in our group to help you," Daniel said.

"It's definitely not going to include you," Izzy replied.

Everyone laughed.

"I can help," Brenda said. "It sounds like we need to do our homework before we interview people. Anything else we need to follow?"

"One more thing." Daniel consulted his notes. "Louise Waldman had a recently filed malpractice suit. We should talk to the plaintiff. It could be that whoever filed the suit was angry enough to take matters into his own hands."

"Seems unlikely," Izzy said. "Aren't these medical malpractice suits all about money? Why kill the goose that might lay your golden egg?"

"It depends on what the suit's about," Brenda said. "And what the result of the alleged malpractice was."

"True on all counts," Daniel said. "But I want us to be thorough. Okay, everyone, grab your last bagel and get going on your assignments. We'll rendezvous again Monday morning and see what we have."

Daniel spread some cream cheese on a sesame bagel, and he and Brenda returned to their adjacent cubicles.

"What are you planning to do this morning?" Brenda asked.

"I want to follow up on a loose end from yesterday. There was an empty storefront in the mini mall near where Louise's car was found. I want to take a look at it."

"Are you thinking she could have met someone there?" Brenda asked.

"Either there or in one of the homes on that street. The storefront is listed by Affordable Realty Corporation."

"Isn't Affordable Realty an oxymoron?" Brenda asked.

Daniel grinned. "Let's find out."

Daniel's call was answered by a real estate agent, who identified himself as Dean Morgan. "I'm interested in the empty storefront you have listed on Pico. I'm looking for some affordable office space."

"We're asking $1500 a month," Morgan said. "Is that in your price range?"

"It is indeed," Daniel replied. "How soon can I see it?"

"How soon can you be here?"

Daniel looked at his watch. "Half an hour."

"I'll meet you out front."

Brenda looked over from her computer and raised her eyebrows. "Are you doing this undercover?"

"For the moment. An empty storefront, late at night, could be a convenient place to hold or kill someone. I'll see what I can find out first, and then decide if the place is worth a crime scene team."

Daniel pulled his car into the mall parking lot and spotted the realtor waiting for him. He was a wholesome, preppy-looking guy, with a blond crew cut, wearing a white shirt under a blue wool pullover, and a neatly pressed pair of khakis. He spotted Daniel and placed a salesman's smile on his face.

"Mr. Ross?" He held out his hand and Daniel shook it.

"I appreciate you meeting me on a Saturday."

"No problem. I live close by," Morgan said. "Let me show you the space."

He opened the door and flipped a light switch. A bank of fluorescent lights lit up the dark room. The storefront was shabby, with dirty gray carpet and off-white walls in need of repainting. There were two cheap, six-foot long office tables in the center of the room surrounded by bridge chairs. The chairs were spaced haphazardly, as if a group of people had been sitting and then stood up and left. A few pencils and pads sat on the table. Daniel noticed a wastebasket with empty paper coffee cups.

"Looks like the previous tenant just had a meeting," Daniel said, glancing at the furniture.

"Actually, the space has been vacant for about two months. I occasionally rent it for a day or two, to groups that need inexpensive conference places," the realtor said.

Daniel's radar was on alert. He kept his hands in his pockets to avoid leaving any fingerprints.

"It needs a little work," he commented. "Will the landlord pay for new carpet and paint? Who is the landlord, by the way?"

"It's an outfit based in Orange County called Smithfield Development. They own the whole mall. We manage it for them, and yes, paint and commercial grade carpet is part of the deal," Morgan answered.

"Is there a bathroom?"

"In the back. I'll show you."

The bathroom was small and dirty. There was a ring of grime in the toilet that suggested it hadn't been flushed for a while.

"This could use an upgrade as well," Daniel said.

"It could be negotiated, if you're interested."

"Well, the rent is right and so is the location," Daniel said. "Let me think about it and get back to you."

Daniel returned to his car, waited for Morgan to leave, and called Brenda.

"I think we need a warrant for the store. It looks like there was a meeting in it recently."

"I've been reviewing the mall security video. There's a clip of Louise walking west in the mall parking lot, but it cut off before I could see exactly where she went. The time was seven twenty-five p.m. And that's where we lose her. She wasn't seen inside the fast food place at the other end," Brenda said.

"I'm on my way back," Daniel said. "Can you find out whether any autopsy or trace evidence results are back yet?"

Brenda laughed. "Dream on."

Brenda waved at Daniel, as he walked into the detective's room at the station.

"No luck," she said. "Even Bill Pincus gets time off on the weekend. We're going to have to wait a few days for results."

Daniel sighed. "Any of you guys find out anything useful?"

"Yeah," said Izzy. "The husband was definitely in New York and on the plane. He also stands to inherit everything in Louise's estate except for her charitable contributions. His will is similar. She would have gotten it all."

"What about the partnership agreement?" Daniel asked.

"It's complicated, but the bottom line is that I don't see any immediate financial gain for any of the partners. In fact, it's the opposite. Her share of the practice will be evaluated and her estate will have to be reimbursed for the hard assets."

"What do you mean by hard assets?" Brenda asked.

"All the expensive medical equipment in the lab, the exam rooms, and the surgical center," Izzy said.

"So only the husband stands to gain from her death," Daniel said. "Does he need the money?"

"I haven't gone into either of their financials in-depth," Izzy said. "I thought I'd start working on her computer next."

"Do we have a warrant yet?" Daniel asked Brenda.

"It isn't that easy to find a friendly judge on a Saturday," she answered. "I'm working on it."

Sometimes, Daniel hated weekends. Hopefully they'd pick up their momentum on Monday.

CHAPTER THIRTEEN

I HAD BEEN LOOKING FORWARD TO THE weekend. Neither Daniel nor I were on call, and we'd promised to take Zoe somewhere fun. The only place I wanted to go at the moment was back to bed, but I couldn't ruin Zoe's Sunday just because I was feeling anxious and depressed. I was torn between resenting Daniel's absence and being glad that he and Brenda were investigating Louise's murder. I knew that he wouldn't rest until it was solved. I needed to vent, so I called my best friend Andrea.

"I'm planning on taking Zoe to the Auto Museum later today," I said. "Would you and Molly like to come with us?"

Molly was Andrea's two-year-old daughter. She was adorable and had the energy of an NFL football team. She adored Zoe and followed her with the devotion of a spaniel. Zoe, for her part, accepted her big sister responsibilities seriously and took good care of Molly. I anticipated she'd be equally devoted to a sibling, should I be successful in my quest.

"Sounds like fun," Andrea said. "How was the egg retrieval?"

I sighed. "My embryos are fine but my doctor isn't. Louise didn't show up for my procedure, and yesterday, her murdered body was found in a dumpster. Daniel and Brenda are investigating."

"Oh, sweetie, I am so sorry," Andrea said. "Sounds like you need a hug and a sympathetic ear. What time shall we pick you up?"

We agreed on 10:30 a.m., and Andrea insisted on driving. She was probably worried that I'd be too distracted to be trusted with two children in the back seat. No doubt, she was right.

Zoe had taken a surprising interest in cool-looking cars. She thought my Toyota was boring, but loved sitting in the driver's seat of Daniel's Mustang. I figured he was going to have to teach her to drive in his car when she reached fifteen.

Andrea arrived precisely on time and honked her horn. Unlike me, my best friend had a love for high-end cars and was driving a Porsche Panamera. I seat-belted Zoe into the back seat next to Molly, and slid into the passenger side. Andrea leaned over, kissed my cheek and squeezed my hand. As usual, she looked gorgeous, with her long, honey-colored hair cascading over her shoulders, not a strand out of place. I was convinced that Andrea's pregnant mother had been first in line on the day God distributed hair.

I knew Andrea had a great many questions, but we couldn't talk about murder in front of the children.

Once we arrived at the museum, we went upstairs to the floor with all the vintage cars. Zoe took Molly by the hand and led her toward a 1993 blue Jaguar XJ 220.

"Mommy, when I'm ready to drive can I have that one?" Zoe pointed to a red Ferrari.

"I'm afraid not, honey," I said. "They don't make that car anymore."

The poor child was clearly going to be doomed to disappointment. I intended to buy her something inexpensive and practical.

Andrea and I followed, closely enough to keep an eye on both kids, but at enough of a distance so we could have a quiet conversation without being overheard. I filled her in on what I knew of the murder and the investigation.

"You must be devastated," she said.

"I know that none of this is my fault, but I keep wondering if I have some sort of bad karma. People who know me keep getting killed." Tears welled up in my eyes and I tried to blot them with my sleeve.

Andrea reached into her voluminous purse and handed me a packet of tissues, standard equipment for a psychiatrist. I blew my nose.

"Sweetie, this isn't like you. It's okay to cry over the loss of your friend, but it's not okay to blame yourself. I know you helped Daniel solve several cases, but the victim wasn't always a person you knew as well as Louise."

I thought about my sister-in-law, Beth, and about Katy, the sweet little girl in my carpool. Those were deaths that left a hole in my heart. The tears kept coming.

"Maybe it's just hormones," I wailed, trying to get myself under control. I didn't want Zoe to see me cry.

Andrea put an arm around me and gave me a hug. "Are you planning to help Daniel this time?" she asked.

I extracted another tissue and blotted my cheeks. The flow subsided.

"Part of me wants desperately to help. The rest of me wants to leave it all to him and to concentrate on getting pregnant and taking care of my patients."

"Maybe you can find a middle ground," she suggested.

"Such as?"

"If you come across useful information in the course of your regular activities, pass it on, but don't make an effort to probe, and for heaven's sake, don't put yourself in danger. You've had a few close calls," Andrea said.

I had experienced some terrifying moments and had no desire to repeat any of them. Andrea's advice felt right to me. I wanted to enjoy planning our wedding and our life together, and I didn't have the time or emotional energy to get deeply involved in a murder investigation.

"You always manage to say the right thing," I said. "I think we'd better catch up to the kids and stop them from climbing inside that 1965 Mustang."

CHAPTER FOURTEEN

D ANIEL GOT HOME SHORTLY AFTER ZOE and I did, and patiently paid attention as she showed him the many photos I'd allowed her to take on my cell phone.

"So, when you turn fifteen and get your driver's license, you'd like a Ferrari?" he said.

"Yup."

"I'd like one too. Maybe I'll let you drive it."

"Planning on winning the Lottery?" I asked.

Daniel grinned.

"Let's order in Thai food," I suggested.

After dinner, with Zoe safely out of earshot, I asked him if there had been any progress and he filled me in.

"Are you going to call Nori Tanaka and break the bad news?"

"No. We're getting a warrant for Louise's office on Monday, and I want to talk to her two partners. I need to see their reactions when I tell them Louise was murdered."

"Do you suspect one of them?" I asked, as I loaded the dishwasher and put away the leftovers.

"I suspect everyone. You know them both. What's your impression?"

The truth was that I didn't like them, but I had trouble visualizing either one as a cold-blooded killer.

"Not my cup of tea."

"Why not?" Daniel asked. "You're usually fairly tolerant."

I thought about it as I put the remaining Pad Thai into a plastic container. "I'm not sure I should answer that now. I don't want to contaminate your first impressions with my feelings. Why don't you interview them first, and then I'll be happy to compare notes. Fair enough?"

"Deal."

"Anything else on your agenda?" I asked.

"Hopefully, we'll have a warrant for the empty storefront soon. I want to collect trace evidence and see if Louise was there. What are you doing tomorrow?"

"Grand Rounds, the office, and I'm supposed to go to a fund raising event tomorrow night."

"Seriously?" Daniel said. "I thought you hated those things."

"I do, but this one is for Planned Parenthood. Louise was on the board."

"Right, and you said you knew the director."

"Frances is an old friend and colleague, and she and Louise were very close. Daniel, I don't know if she's even heard about Louise. There hasn't been any media coverage yet. Can I tell her?"

"You were there when we all realized she was missing and it'll be in the news pretty quickly. I wouldn't be surprised if the grapevine spreads the information long before you attend that event," he said.

"I take it that's a yes."

Daniel put an arm around me and drew me close. I rested my head on his chest and took a deep breath.

"Tomorrow's going to be a tough day for a lot of people," he said.

Grand Rounds took place every Monday morning and allowed me to keep up with some of my continuing medical education, and to occasionally socialize with colleagues I wouldn't otherwise see. As I stood in line for a cup of tepid coffee, I felt a hand on my shoulder.

"Hannah, good morning."

I turned around. Ian Price, one of Louise's partners, was standing behind me.

"I heard you were at our office on Friday, when Louise failed to show up. Have you heard anything further?"

"I haven't," I replied. "Have you?"

Ian was looking at me with an expression of concern on his handsome face. He was wearing scrubs and a white coat, his thick gray hair artfully tousled, a gold Rolex visible on the wrist of his other hand, which held a paper plate and a bran muffin. I could see his appeal to vulnerable female patients. I wasn't one of them.

"I thought you had the inside track at the LAPD," he said.

"I'm afraid not. Daniel isn't allowed to discuss an ongoing investigation."

"Are you joining us Wednesday night?" he asked. "We're having a dinner and presentation on surrogacy."

"I'm not sure I can make it," I hedged. "But I'll let you know."

Clearly, his inner entrepreneur had resurfaced. How the

guy could be promoting a practice-building dinner, when his senior partner was missing, astonished me. I wondered if he would cancel it once he learned the truth.

As I sat in the auditorium, I praised myself for my restraint. I'd kept my mouth shut and hadn't interfered with Daniel's interview plans for later that morning.

———————

CHAPTER FIFTEEN

A T 7:30 A.M., DANIEL ENTERED THE police conference room with a brief agenda in mind. "Good morning everyone. Let's get to it. Jason, any results from the canvassing you did over the weekend?"

"Nope. See no evil, hear no evil, speak no evil."

"Did you miss anyone?" Daniel asked.

"Most folks were home on Saturday. The few that weren't, we interviewed on Sunday. No one admits to knowing anything, although of course, someone could be lying."

"Brenda, where are we with the search warrants?"

Brenda smiled. "I got them both, the storefront and Louise's office."

Noting a few puzzled looks, Daniel recounted his activities on Saturday afternoon. "We need to collect trace evidence to see if Louise was murdered in the empty store, and find out who was using the space for a meeting. Brenda, can you handle that this morning?"

"Sure."

"I'm going to Louise's office," Daniel continued, "to interview her partners and confiscate her office computer and papers. Izzy, did you find anything useful on Louise's home computer?"

Izzy frowned. "Yes and no. Her email and browsing history were innocuous until I discovered a program that she didn't keep on her desktop. It's a browser called Tor."

"Is that supposed to mean something to me?" Daniel asked.

"Not to you," Izzy commented. "But Brenda probably knows what it is. People use Tor, not only to send encrypted content, which you can do with any browser, but to obscure their traffic pattern."

Daniel ran his hands through his hair. "I have a bad feeling about this. Tor works how?"

"It routes your emails, or your connection to a website, through several encrypted servers to make it impossible for anyone to connect you to the final destination. It also makes it impossible for people at the receiving end to pinpoint your location."

"Is this the browser that Homeland Security is so unhappy about?" Jason asked.

"One of them," Izzy said. "Tor is a favorite browser for spies, terrorists and anyone else who wants to keep their web activities absolutely private. If Louise was using it, she was hiding something important. The bad news is, I can't hack it."

"Great," Daniel said. "Another roadblock. Okay, everyone, let's get going. I want to reach Louise's office before any patients get there."

Daniel and two techs from the evidence team reached the offices of Westside Fertility Associates at 8:45 a.m. The door was locked, but his knock was answered by the receptionist he'd met on Friday.

"Is Dr. Tanaka in?" he asked.

"I'll get her for you."

"Thanks," Daniel said. "Perhaps we could wait in Dr. Waldman's office? I don't want to disturb your patients."

The receptionist led them back to Louise's consultation room, and left to find Dr. Tanaka.

"Should we get started?" one of the techs asked.

"Not yet. I want to give Dr. Tanaka the news first and the search warrant."

It was only a moment later when Nori entered the office, dressed in scrubs with a blue paper hat, a surgical mask hanging around her neck.

"Have you found her?" she asked.

"I'm afraid so," Daniel said. "We found her body in a construction dumpster near the 10 Freeway. She was murdered."

"Oh, God." Nori Tanaka covered her face with her hands, and turned away from him so he couldn't see her cry, but her shoulders shook.

"I'm so sorry. We'll do whatever we can to find whoever killed her." Daniel said, and waited for her to regain her composure.

Finally, she turned around and looked at him. "What now?"

"These two gentlemen are evidence technicians. We have a warrant for Louise's office. I need to collect her computer and papers to see if they can shed any light on what happened." He handed over the warrant. "Don't worry. Patient records are excluded from the warrant."

"Okay." Nori backed away toward the door.

"Would you like me to come with you when you notify your staff?" Daniel asked.

"No, thanks. I'll tell them. You find out who killed Louise."

"I need to interview your other two partners. Are they in yet?"

"Dr. Nazari just finished a seven-thirty case. I'll introduce you."

Kaspar Nazari was a dark, handsome man in his early thirties, with an impressive mustache. He was wearing scrubs, had short, gelled hair, and was nursing a mug of coffee at his desk.

"Kaspar, this is Detective Daniel Ross of the LAPD. He wants a word with you," Nori said.

Nazari sprang to his feet, offered his hand, and exhibited a dazzling display of white teeth. "Sit down, Detective. Any word on Dr. Waldman?"

Nori slipped out of the room, closing the door quietly and leaving the two men alone.

Daniel took a seat and broke the news.

The smile vanished. "That's tragic. Do the police have any idea of who killed her?"

"We're just beginning our investigation," Daniel said. "I have some questions."

"Of course. I'll do anything to help." Nazari leaned back in his chair.

"When someone dies," Daniel said, "people are often reluctant to say anything negative about them, but what helps us the most in our investigations is a clear picture of who the victim was. You can help by giving me your honest impression of Dr. Waldman."

"What do you want to know?" Nazari asked.

"What was she like as a doctor, a colleague, an employer? Did people like her or were there reasons someone might have a grudge against her?"

Nazari clasped his hands and chewed on his lower lip for a moment as he considered the question. "You want my honest assessment?"

"I do."

"Louise Waldman was an excellent physician. She kept up with all the scientific advances in our field and contributed a considerable amount of research. She was always careful, ethical, conscientious with her patients and well liked."

"And?" Daniel said.

"As an employer, she was strict and had very high standards," Nazari continued. "She didn't tolerate laziness or lack of attention to detail. I believe some of the staff were a little afraid of her and found her micromanaging annoying."

"Annoying enough to want to kill her?" Daniel asked. "Was there anyone she fired who might have held a grudge?"

"I don't think so. Most of our staff has been here for a long time. She was fair, and she paid well. They would have found it difficult to find a better job."

"What was she like as a colleague?" Daniel asked.

"Louise was the senior partner. She wasn't a very good business woman. She was always too cautious, unwilling to take big steps to expand the practice. You know how women are."

"How are they?"

"They can't see the big picture. We could have been

making a lot more money if it hadn't been for her stubbornness. Ian and I had to push her hard just to get her to agree to open a second office in the Valley. She was always worried about us overextending ourselves financially. There's no profit without risk."

"What will happen to the practice with Dr. Waldman gone?" Daniel asked.

"I don't know. The partners will have to discuss it."

"Can you tell me when you last saw her?"

"It was probably on Tuesday. She's off on Wednesdays, and I'm at our Valley office on Thursday."

"Did you have any sense that she was worried? Was there anything unusual about her behavior?"

Nazari shrugged. "We didn't really talk to one another very much. I wouldn't have noticed."

"When you finished at your office in the Valley, Thursday night, where did you go?"

"Home to have dinner with my family. Why?"

"I'm just checking on people's whereabouts, the night she was killed." Daniel stood up. "Thank you, Dr. Nazari. I'll let you know if I have any more questions."

Nazari came out from behind his desk and walked Daniel to the door.

"Certainly, Detective." He flashed his dazzling smile again. "Any time."

Daniel closed the door behind him. It was time to check in with the forensic team, and he still needed to see if Ian Price was finally available.

Daniel and Brenda reconvened at the station early that afternoon.

"How was your morning?" Daniel asked.

"I brought you lots of fingerprints and coffee cups with DNA from the storefront, and the contact information for the guy who rented the space from Affordable Real Estate. Do you want to go see him?"

"Not yet. Let's see if there's any evidence that Louise was actually there. Let's research the guy first and see who else's fingerprints show up. Izzy, you got anything new for us? I've got her office computer and records for you."

"I checked out Hank Waldman's financials and his phone record," Izzy said. "The guy's loaded. If he was involved with killing his wife, it wasn't for money, and I couldn't find anything suspicious in the phone records. I think you guys should look elsewhere for now."

"Thanks," Daniel said.

"What did you find out from the partners?" Brenda asked.

"I figured out why Hannah doesn't like them. They're both a bit full of themselves, and obviously resented Louise's senior status. They thought her caution was holding them back from making the big bucks."

"Enough resentment for a motive to kill?"

"I'm not ready to cross either one of them off my list. Neither one has an airtight alibi for Thursday night."

"So, what do you want to do while we're waiting for the forensics?" Brenda asked.

"We can check out the plaintiff in that malpractice suit."

"Not the lawyer?"

"He won't talk to us. He'll just cite the usual bullshit about client confidentiality. The plaintiff's name is Phillip Bachman. He owns a small gym, not far from here on Santa Monica Boulevard. Let's grab some lunch and go see him."

The Basic-Fit Gym was one of a chain of low-priced, bare-bones facilities scattered around Los Angeles. This one was just east of the 405 Freeway. From the street, one could get a panoramic view of the interior with its rows of bikes, ellipticals and treadmills facing the glass windows. At this hour, the gym was sparsely populated.

Daniel and Brenda approached the receptionist and asked to speak to Mr. Bachman. She waved them toward the back where a man was lying on a weight bench, holding up a heavy barbell.

"Mr. Bachman?" Daniel asked.

He sat up. "That's me. What can I do for you?"

From a distance, Bachman looked like a thirty-year-old. His tight t-shirt revealed a well-developed six-pack and bulging biceps. A closer look, however, suggested that he was pushing sixty. His face was sun-damaged and wrinkled, with bushy, dark brows. What was left of his hair was gray and close-cropped around a shiny, bald dome.

"I'm Detective Daniel Ross, and this is my partner, Detective Jordan. May we have a word? We're working on a case, and your name came up. We thought you might be able to help us."

"What case?"

"It concerns Dr. Louise Waldman," Brenda said.

"Someone else sue her? About time," Bachman said. "Come on back to my office."

The office was the size of a generous utility closet and cluttered with papers and cartons. Bachman sat at his desk and motioned Daniel and Brenda to take a seat on a weight bench opposite it.

"So, what did she do?" he asked.

"Your name came up as a plaintiff in a malpractice action against her. Can you tell us what that was about?" Daniel said.

"Breach of contract," Bachman answered. "My wife, Vicki, and I consulted her because Vicki was over forty and having trouble getting pregnant. We decided to try in-vitro fertilization and signed a contract that said, in the event of divorce, any embryos we had in storage would be destroyed."

"Are you getting a divorce?" Brenda asked.

"It's in process," he said. "Louise Waldman impregnated Vicki after the divorce papers were filed and now she's having twins. I refuse to be on the hook for lifetime child support for two brats I didn't want. I'm suing Waldman."

"Did Dr. Waldman know you were divorcing?" Brenda asked.

He shrugged. "I told my lawyer to notify her office."

"I see. So, when was the last time you saw or spoke to Dr. Waldman?" Daniel asked.

"Vicki and I went to see Dr. Waldman together about five months ago. Two months later, we decided having a baby wasn't going to save a bad marriage, and decided to split up."

"And you've had no contact of any kind since that initial visit?" Brenda persisted.

"Why would I contact her? That's my lawyer's job. He's going to make sure she pays big time."

"Thank you, Mr. Bachman. We appreciate your help," Daniel said.

"Aren't you going to tell me what else the bitch has done?" Bachman asked.

"Sorry," Brenda said. "We can't comment on an ongoing investigation."

"I guess that's a dead end," Brenda said as they walked out the door.

"True, but he sure seems to hate her," Daniel said.

"I wonder if Louise Waldman knew about the pending divorce before she completed the in vitro on Mrs. Bachman. Maybe the lawyer dropped the ball."

"From what I've learned about Louise, I can't imagine she would have proceeded if she'd known. No doctor wants a malpractice suit," Daniel said.

"I wonder what happens to the lawsuit now that Louise is dead?"

"He can probably sue her estate," Daniel said. "I wonder if we should have told him?"

Brenda shrugged.

This discussion reminded Daniel that tomorrow was the big day. Hannah was going in to have the embryo implanted into her uterus. He hoped she'd arrive home early from that fundraiser tonight, and be pregnant by mid-morning.

CHAPTER SIXTEEN

FORTUNATELY, THE PLANNED Parenthood fundraiser wasn't a dinner. There are few things I find more difficult when I'm tired and depressed than trying to make cheerful conversation at a table of strangers. I've never been any good at working a room.

The event was a celebration of the opening of Planned Parenthood's newest facility on the Westside of town and consisted of wine, snack food, and tours of the premises. It really was quite a nice clinic. The exam and operating rooms were fitted with the latest equipment, and the waiting room was spacious and decorated in soft, soothing colors and comfortable furniture. The place exuded warmth and caring. They'd obviously gotten some major donations to build the facility.

I helped myself to a glass of white wine and circulated, chatting with hospital colleagues and keeping an eye out for Frances Conners, the Medical Director. I finally spotted her in a corner, making animated conversation with a heavyset gentleman. I drifted in her direction.

Frances was Irish and in her fifties. She could have been

lifted out of a PBS English village with her fair skin, blue eyes, snub nose, and short, extremely curly, gray hair. Although I always imagined her in a twinset and tweeds, tonight, she was wearing a polished cotton print shirtwaist dress. Her somewhat dowdy appearance was deceptive. She was way smarter and tougher than she looked.

As the heavyset gentleman moved away, I took his place, depositing my empty glass on a nearby table, and offering her both my hands in greeting.

"Beautiful facility, Frances." I said.

"Thank you."

She gave me a long, thoughtful look, made up her mind and proceeded. "It's a bittersweet celebration. I assume you've heard about Louise's death."

"I have," I said. "I know what close friends you were. You must be devastated."

"We're all in shock," Frances said. "We considered cancelling tonight, but decided to proceed as a tribute to her. She put so much of her time, effort and energy into this organization, not to mention a huge donation toward the new building."

"Is there someplace more private we can talk?" I asked, as the crowd got larger.

"Come with me."

I followed her past the operating rooms and into her office. At her gesture, I took a seat.

"I've known Louise for years," I said. "It's so hard to imagine that anyone would want to kill her. You were a close personal friend. Do you know of someone who hated her?"

"Louise wasn't the sort of person to inspire hate."

"Do the initials FPA mean anything to you?"

Her face went white. "Why are you asking?"

"My fiancé, Daniel, is the LAPD detective in charge of

investigating her death. He asked me if I knew what the abbreviation meant, because it was in her calendar on the day she died, and on several other days. I have no clue."

"I can't believe she actually did it," Frances said.

"Did what?"

"FPA stands for Fetal Protection Association. It's a California-based, radical right-wing, anti-abortion group that is an offshoot of the Center for Medical Progress, the organization that produced those doctored videos claiming that Planned Parenthood sold fetal tissue for profit."

"What's that got to do with Louise?" I asked.

"Louise was furious about the videos. She said we should infiltrate some of these groups and find out what they're up to. If they can secretly record us, we should be able to do the same. I thought she was just sounding off. I never imagined she'd do something about it."

I visualized her date book in my mind. FPA, 7:30 p.m., on Thursdays, for three months.

I stared at Frances. "Do you think she was going to meetings, undercover?"

"If she was, maybe she blew her cover," Frances said.

"Louise always struck me as such a cautious, careful person. I can't imagine her playing secret agent."

"You didn't know her as well as I did," Frances said. "She was quite the adventurer when we were in college. Louise loved extreme sports. She skied black diamond slopes, went snowboarding and hang gliding. I would have been terrified to do the things she did, but Louise was turned on by the thrill of risking her life."

"You're saying that infiltrating a dangerous right-wing organization would have excited her?"

"I'm afraid so," Frances said. "It makes perfect sense to me."

"I've got to tell Daniel about this. Don't say anything to anyone."

"I won't," she said, troubled.

We both headed for the door. Just before we got there, we stopped and hugged one another for a long time.

When I got home, Daniel was in the den, in his favorite chair, with a book. Zoe was curled up in a fetal position, on the sofa, sound asleep.

"You're home early," he whispered. "I was going to carry her to her room as soon as I finished this chapter."

"Did you two have a fun evening?" I asked.

"Pizza and two movies."

"No homework?"

Daniel grinned. "Homework first."

I put my purse and briefcase on a table, and bent down to offer him a kiss.

He got up and lifted Zoe into his arms. She rested her head on his shoulder. I followed him into her room, pulling back the covers on her bed and tucking her in. She didn't wake as we tiptoed out.

"How was the fundraiser?" he asked.

"I can describe it in three words," I said. "Fetal Protection Association."

<h1 style="text-align:center">CHAPTER SEVENTEEN</h1>

Daniel got to the station early on Tuesday morning to meet with his team.

"We've got a break in the case," he announced. "FPA stands for Fetal Protection Association, a bunch of radical pro-lifers. We think Louise was going to meetings under-cover to find out what they were up to."

"How'd you find that out?" Jason asked.

"Hannah. She went to a Planned Parenthood fundraiser. Louise was on the board. Hannah asked the medical director if she had any idea of what the initials stood for."

"We should put Hannah on salary," Brenda said.

"Anything back on the forensics?" Daniel asked. "Do we have any evidence that Louise was in that storefront?"

"Not yet," Izzy said. "But there's a phone message for you to call the lab."

Daniel reached for his cell phone, while Izzy started a computer search.

"It's Detective Ross. You called?"

"Yeah, I did. This is James in the lab. I've got something

interesting for you. Remember that bottle of Aqua Fina you turned in from the vic's car?"

"What about it?"

"It isn't a water bottle. It's a hidden camera. The lens is behind the label and there are water compartments above and below so you can actually drink out of it."

"No shit?" Daniel said.

"I've transferred the data to a DVD for you. I'll send it over to the conference room now."

Daniel ended the call, feeling optimistic. He had to hand it to Louise. A water bottle. That was ingenious.

"Daniel, you've got to see this," Izzy said.

Daniel walked over. "What's going on?"

"This site has a comprehensive list of all the abortion clinics and providers in Southern California with pictures, addresses and phone numbers. It's like a whole bunch of little Wanted Posters, so that the bastards can target doctors. Hannah is on it."

Daniel peered over Izzy's shoulder at the screen. There was a photo of Hannah, copied from the Memorial Hospital website, along with her office information. A shiver ran down his spine and his rage started to build.

CHAPTER EIGHTEEN

I HAD TAKEN THE MORNING OFF FROM the office. I was hoping to get pregnant today and figured that a little post-implantation relaxation wouldn't hurt. Daniel had planned to come with me, but I told him not to.

"This doesn't involve any anesthesia," I'd explained. "And I can drive myself there and to my office afterwards. You go catch the bastard who killed Louise."

"Yes, ma'am," Daniel had said, drawing me into his arms. "You go make our baby."

I arrived at Westside Fertility Associates at the appointed time and greeted the receptionist. Usually, she had a big smile for me, but today, her face was grim.

"How are you all holding up?" I asked.

She shook her head. "The whole office is a mess. People are still crying in the lunch room."

"I know," I said, reaching over to squeeze her hand. "It's horrible."

"Dr. Tanaka is ready for you, Dr. Kline. Why don't you go on back to her consult room?"

Nori was at her desk and attempted a smile as I walked in.

"Have a seat," she said. "I just want to review one or two things before we do the embryo transfer."

"How are my eggs?" I asked.

"We retrieved twelve and fertilized them. Six have developed into very nice embryos. As you requested, we ran prenatal genetic diagnosis on them and had to discard three for chromosome abnormalities. That's pretty common at your age."

I knew. Fertility was all downhill from thirty-five on.

"I assume you discussed this with Louise, but I just want to confirm your choice," Nori continued. "Because of the problems with multiple births, the standard of practice has become implanting only one embryo. In women over forty, however, we go as high as two, in order to increase the odds that at least one will take hold. This would, however, result in possible twins. Are you ready for that?"

Daniel and I had already had that discussion. Our lives were complex enough with two difficult jobs and finding time for Zoe. We thought we could manage two children, but three sounded overwhelming to us both.

"We've talked about it," I said. "We'll take our chances with one embryo at a time."

"Any preference as to sex?" Nori asked.

"I don't like the idea of using this technology for sex selection, unless there's a sex-linked genetic disorder. Just implant the best looking embryo we've got. All I care about is a normal baby."

"All right, then," Nori said. "Let's get started."

CHAPTER NINETEEN

D ANIEL LOOKED OVER AT IZZY. "GO ahead and start that DVD."

Izzy slipped the disc into the player and asked Jason to turn off the room light. On the flat screen TV, the picture was initially blurred. There was a view of ceiling tiles and fluorescent lights.

"Maybe she's drinking from the bottle," Jason suggested.

When the picture cleared, Daniel recognized the storefront interior. The lights were dim and shades covered the glass-front windows. There were five people seated at the table. At the head, was a bald, obese man, with a thick gray beard and steel-rimmed glasses. At the other end, sat a young woman with a horsey face, no makeup and lank brown hair, wearing a white blouse with a Peter Pan collar. There were three younger men, all similar in appearance: buzz cuts, T shirts, extensive tattoos on their arms.

"Looks like a white supremacist fashion show," Brenda commented.

"We should get close ups of the tattoos, and see if there are any gang ID's," Izzy said.

The obese man began to speak. "You all know what our problem is here in Los Angeles. Unlike most other places, abortions aren't just done in clinics that we can target. They're spread out all over. Doctors do them for their patients in the privacy of their offices, and don't advertise."

"Karen-Kay over there," he pointed to the young woman, "has been doing great work over the past few months, calling doctor's offices, pretending to need an abortion and finding out who does them. She's really expanded our database."

"We're ready for our next step," Karen-Kay said. "We need to send a much stronger message."

"We do, indeed," the obese man said. Our friends here," he looked over at the three younger men, "are building us a few bombs which can be detonated with a cell phone. Karen-Kay and Mildred can make appointments for a pap smear, leave the bombs in the exam rooms, and detonate them after they leave."

"That won't work." It was Louise's voice. "You're looking at a public relations disaster for the pro-life movement. You blow up an ob-gyn office, you're going to kill or injure a bunch of pregnant women who are getting prenatal care and who want their babies. How pro-life is that?"

The man stroked his beard. "Mildred has a point."

"We could wait until after office hours to detonate," Karen-Kay said. "That way, we just do property damage, and if we're really lucky, the doctor will still be there doing paperwork."

"Right," said one of the young guys. "You murder the murderer and justice is served."

"How long before the bombs are ready to go?" the older man asked.

"Almost ready now."

"Good. You two girls, pick your targets from the database and make appointments. Don't tell us or one another who the targets are. I'll let you know where to pick up the bombs. Here's a burner phone for each of you."

"All right," Louise said. Her hand reached out and took a phone from him. The picture went dark.

"She must have put the bottle back in her purse," Daniel said.

"I need to go," Louise's voice said. "I'll be ready when you call."

There was a sound of footsteps, and a door opening and closing, then nothing.

"Jeez," Jason said.

"Izzy, can you get to work with a facial recognition program?"

"Right away."

"The fat man looks like the description of Carl Smith, the guy the realtor said rented the storefront," Brenda said.

"Smith?" Daniel said. "Sounds like a pseudonym to me."

"I agree," Brenda said. "But let me see if there's a DMV driver's license in that name with a matching picture. If not, we'll have to rely on Izzy and the fingerprints."

"Brenda, go back and check out the surveillance videos from the mini-mall. See if you can find Louise leaving and any of those guys following her," Daniel said.

"I'm on it."

"I also need you to run a photo of that woman, Karen-Kay, and get me a handful of copies" Daniel said. "I have to alert Hannah's office."

"We need to do more than alert Hannah," Brenda said. "She's not the only doctor in town doing abortions in their office. This falls under the rubric of terrorism. We have to notify the FBI."

CHAPTER TWENTY

As a rule, Daniel hated working with the FBI. The moment he called them in on a case, they behaved as if he worked for them and they were in charge. However, he had to admit that Brenda was right. This was terrorism. The FBI had access to resources that were not available to the LAPD, and preventing this attack was too important for jurisdictional disputes. He picked up the phone.

When Daniel left the conference room, he found Brenda hunched over her computer, reviewing security tapes. He peered over her shoulder.

"Did you talk to the Feds?" she asked.

"They're sending over a couple of agents to meet with us this afternoon. I encrypted the video and emailed it to them. Have you found anything more on the tapes?"

"Yes and no," Brenda said. "Take a look. Here's one from the falafel place next door to the storefront. It has a view of the parking lot. Here's Louise at ten-thirty p.m., walking east."

Brenda switched views to another camera. "This one's

from the furniture store. She's walking quickly and seems nervous, looking over her shoulder and reaching into her handbag."

Brenda zoomed in on a view of Louise's hand, opening the outer flap on her shoulder bag and retrieving a set of keys. "It looks like she's on her way to her car and wants to get into it ASAP."

"Is that the last we see of her?" Daniel asked.

"Yes. The furniture store is at the east end of the mall. She was parked around the corner."

"Did you see any of those guys following her?"

"I saw them all leave, and none of them went in her direction." She fast forwarded to 10:43 p.m. "Here are the skinheads. One of them got on a motorcycle, and the other two got into a black Ford F-150 truck about five minutes later. They all went west, toward the freeway. I asked Izzy to check out the traffic cameras on Pico, to see if we can follow them."

"Were you able to get license numbers?"

"Got one for the truck. I traced it to a stolen Toyota Corolla. No joy there."

"What about our friends, Carl and Karen-Kay?"

Brenda fast-forwarded two minutes. The two of them walked out of the storefront and got into the same car, a silver Chevy Corvette, headed west.

"That's a pretty conspicuous car for a terrorist," Daniel commented.

"Maybe he's having a midlife crisis. Sports car and a much younger woman," Brenda said, rolling her eyes.

"Did you get a license on that one?"

"I was just looking when you got here," she said.

"Carry on. I'm taking an early lunch and stopping in at

Hannah's office to check for bombs. I'm also going to make damn sure that the Feds don't exclude us from investigating Louise's murder."

CHAPTER TWENTY-ONE

COMPARED TO EGG RETRIEVAL, implantation was painless. Nori insisted that I rest half an hour, and then I drove to the office. I hadn't scheduled patients until the afternoon, so I was working my way through my hospital emails and phone messages when Daniel called.

"You free for lunch?" he asked.

"I'd planned on yogurt at my desk," I answered. "But I could be persuaded."

"I'm not sure I have time to take you anywhere, but I do need to talk to you. I'll be over in twenty minutes."

This was not typical Daniel behavior. I had a hunch he'd learned something about Louise, and wanted to tell me. Twenty minutes later, my receptionist announced that he was in the waiting room. I opened the door to my office and motioned for him to come in. He closed the door and slipped his arms around me.

"Are we pregnant?" he asked.

I laughed. "You'll have to be a little more patient. The pregnancy test won't turn positive for several days, and until we see a heartbeat on the six-week ultrasound, we won't know for sure if we've succeeded."

"Patience isn't either of our strong suits," he said.

"You didn't come all the way across town just for a hug," I said. "You've learned something."

Daniel's face turned serious and he drew me over to the sofa, so we could sit down.

"The LAPD is very appreciative," he said. "Your information was the break in the case that we needed."

"Was Louise attending their meetings?" I asked.

"Not only was she attending them, but she had a hidden camera. It was in her car, disguised as a water bottle."

"Unreal," I said. "You think you know someone you've worked with for years, and then they do something that makes you realize you didn't have a clue as to who they were."

"You didn't think Louise was the type to infiltrate a terrorist organization?"

"Did you?"

Daniel shook his head and removed a photograph from his briefcase.

"I came by to show this to you and your staff. Have you ever seen this woman in your office?"

I reached over and examined the face. It wasn't familiar.

"Who is she?" I asked.

"Why don't you ask your staff to come in here, and Ruth as well. That way I won't have to repeat myself."

My partner, Ruth Silverman, was standing at the front desk, writing out a prescription, while our receptionist was checking out the last of her morning patients. I waited until the patient exited the waiting room.

"Don't go anywhere," I said. "Daniel has some important information for our office."

Ruth looked at her watch. "I have a committee meeting in ten minutes."

"This outranks a committee meeting," Daniel said.

I locked the outside door and motioned everyone into my office. Daniel pulled out the photograph and passed it around.

"This woman is a member of a radical right-wing anti-abortion group. She's been calling local offices pretending to need an abortion, in order to find out who's doing them in the community, and posting that information on her group's website. It's called the Fetal Protection Association. Hannah and Ruth, both of you are listed."

"Seriously?" Ruth said. "That's creepy."

"It's also dangerous," Daniel said. "We have information that this woman is planning to make a routine appointment at the office of someone who performs abortions, in order to hide a bomb that she can detonate remotely. Have any of you seen this woman, or gotten a recent phone call from someone who didn't make an appointment but was asking about abortion services?"

"I got a call like that last week," my receptionist said. "She asked a lot of questions about our procedure and the cost, and then said she hadn't made up her mind yet whether to terminate."

"Did she give a name?" Daniel asked.

"She probably did, but I don't remember."

"This woman's first name is Karen-Kay. I don't know her last name, but she wouldn't necessarily use her real name to make an appointment. Do either of you have a patient coming in by that name?"

"We always verify insurance information first," Ruth said. "It would be hard to leave a fake name."

"Unless she was paying cash," I suggested.

I went to my computer and searched our appointment files for a Karen-Kay. No hits.

"I'm meeting with the FBI this afternoon. They will be warning every abortion provider on the website. In the meantime, make a copy of this photo, and if you see this woman, or if someone you suspect is Karen-Kay makes an appointment, I need to know immediately," Daniel said.

"You got it," Ruth stood up and slung her purse over her shoulder. "I've got to admit, this was far more interesting than my Transfusion Committee meeting."

The rest of the staff followed her out of the office, no doubt eager for lunch. I, on the other hand, had lost my appetite.

"Do you think these people killed Louise?" I asked Daniel.

"I wish it was that straightforward," he answered. "At the moment, I don't have any evidence to support that. All of them left the meeting after she did and drove in the opposite direction."

"Maybe they had someone already waiting near her car," I suggested.

"Possible," Daniel said. "All options are still on the table. In the meantime, so that I don't worry about you this afternoon, I want to search your office."

CHAPTER TWENTY-TWO

D ANIEL MADE IT BACK TO THE STATION ten minutes before the FBI arrived. He had just enough time to assemble his team in the conference room, when two federal agents walked in. They introduced themselves as Brian Anderson and Isabelle Russo.

Anderson looked to be in his forties, tall, fit, sandy hair (what was left of it), and a compensating mustache. Russo appeared to be about ten years younger, with olive skin, black eyes, and a prominent nose suggesting a Southern Italian ancestry. Russo was carrying a tan leather briefcase, from which she removed several files.

"We know this crowd," Anderson said. "We've been watching them for a while. Your undercover agent, Mildred, did a good job. Now we can arrest them."

"She wasn't our undercover agent," Daniel said. "She was a physician, Louise Waldman. She acted on her own, and now she's dead."

"Shit," Anderson said. "You think these guys killed her?"

"We don't know," Brenda said. "Surveillance cameras caught all of them leaving the meeting and none of them followed her. We traced their vehicles to the 405 Freeway entrance. The three young guys went north. The two others were in the same car and headed south."

"Were you able to identify them?" Daniel asked.

Russo picked up the files. "The old guy is named Karl Schmidt. He lives in Anaheim and he's the pastor of some right-wing, evangelical church down there. We've had someone attend services. The guy is racist, homophobic and virulently anti-abortion."

"What about Karen-Kay? She his girlfriend?" Brenda asked. "Those types like younger women."

Anderson shook his head. "She's his daughter."

"Who are the skinheads?" Daniel asked.

Russo passed the files around. "They're all ex-military and experienced with explosives. One of them has a history of assault and domestic violence. The other two were just released after being inside for armed robbery. They're all card-carrying members of the Aryan Nation."

"Do they go to Schmidt's church?" Izzy asked.

"I doubt it," Anderson said. "They live up in Canyon Country. I'm not sure how ideological they are about abortion. I think they may just be paid muscle."

"You know where to find them?" Brenda asked.

"One of them owns a ranch that belonged to his parents. The other two are working there. Plenty of room for a little bomb factory. We'll get a SWAT team out there and search the place."

"What if Karen-Kay's already gotten the bomb and made herself an appointment?" Brenda asked.

"We've made a list of all the abortion doctors on their website. We're sending agents to every office, with her picture, to search for any sign of her or explosives," Russo said. "Some of the offices are in Orange County, so we'll need to coordinate with the local FBI office. Although I doubt Karen-Kay's had time to plant a bomb. When have any of you ever gotten an immediate appointment with a doctor?"

"I hope you're right," Brenda said. "You guys want us to go pick up the Schmidt family?"

Anderson shook his head. "Domestic terrorism is our jurisdiction. We've got it."

"We need to be in on the interviews," Daniel said. "We're in the middle of a murder investigation."

"Do you guys think Mildred blew her cover, and the group may have changed plans because of it?" Russo asked.

Daniel shrugged. "If they knew she wasn't legitimate, my bet is that they killed her. If they didn't know, they must be wondering why they haven't heard from her."

"Could they have seen the news about her death and made the connection?" Anderson asked.

"Doubtful," Brenda said. "There was an article inside the California section of the LA Times, but there wasn't a picture."

"Let us know as soon as you've arrested them," Daniel said.

"You got it," Anderson said. "We'll call you when we have the bastards."

"It can't be soon enough for me. My fiancé's practice is on their website and I'm not thrilled at the thought that someone wants to blow up her office."

"So, this is personal for you," Russo said.

"Very."

"Don't let your feelings get in the way of our investigation, Detective," Anderson said.

CHAPTER TWENTY-THREE

I PACED AROUND THE OFFICE ALL afternoon, remembering Daniel's thorough search of our exam rooms and bathrooms, the only locations where patients were left alone and had the privacy to hide something. Daniel hadn't been satisfied until he had searched each one and found nothing.

Most of my patients that afternoon were obstetrical and I saw them on autopilot, checking blood pressure, listening for the fetal heartbeat, measuring the uterus, performing ultrasounds, and answering many of the same questions, multiple times. It was familiar and comfortable, and eventually calmed me down.

My last patient of the day was a new OB named Victoria Bachman. My nurse showed her into my consult room. According to the intake information on my computer, she was forty-three years old. A superficial glance suggested she was about thirty, but this was Beverly Hills, and I knew better.

"A pleasure to meet you," I said. "Congratulations. I see you're having twins. Did you, by any chance, bring me copies of your medical records?"

Victoria brushed a stray lock of beautifully styled, bleached-blonde hair from her face and shook her head. "I had my last appointment scheduled with my fertility doctor last week, but she died unexpectedly, and I wasn't able to get copies. Very inconvenient, but I'm sure we can send for them."

She didn't seem at all distressed at the death of her physician. I noticed that her face barely moved when she talked. No doubt, the lack of wrinkles and mobility was due to Botox. I also suspected that her lush, full lips had been enhanced with filler.

"You must have been Dr. Waldman's patient," I said.

"Dr. Waldman gave me your name, so I could set up an appointment as soon as she was sure the babies were okay."

"Did she also refer you for genetic testing?" I asked. "We normally have any patient over the age of thirty-five tested."

"I have an appointment for the end of the week."

I quickly skimmed through the medical history my nurse had entered into the record. "It seems as if you have no major medical problems that could affect the pregnancy. Is there anything you think I should know before we examine you?"

"Just one thing," Victoria said. "My soon-to-be ex-husband is suing Dr. Waldman for implanting me with our embryos. They were supposed to have been destroyed in the event of divorce, and he is very annoyed that I am pregnant with twins. Good luck to him with the lawsuit now."

She flashed a smug smile.

I took a breath and clenched my fists before responding. "Did Dr. Waldman know you were getting a divorce?"

"Of course not. Why would I have told her? I just thought you should know, in case it ever goes to court and they want you as a witness. I assume our conversations are protected by medical confidentiality."

I was really beginning to dislike this woman. It wasn't a good omen for a doctor-patient relationship. Medical records could be subpoenaed. I hope she wasn't under the illusion that I would perjure myself under oath.

"Why don't we go into the exam room and ultrasound those twins?"

I wondered if Daniel had already interviewed Victoria's soon-to-be ex-husband. I recalled discovering the lawsuit when he asked me to review Louise's calendar. I couldn't imagine that the ex would have had a motive for murdering Louise, although I could see one for murdering Victoria. She was certainly annoying.

When I finally finished with her exam, I retreated to my office. I had yet to process the information about Louise. Who had she been, really? How could I have known her for so long and been so mistaken about her? It must have taken incredible courage to go undercover, and some recklessness as well. I don't know if I could have deliberately exposed myself to that kind of danger, no matter how dedicated I felt to a cause.

Maybe it would be useful to see what I could find out about Louise's past. If the anti-abortion organization hadn't murdered her, perhaps there was a clue in her history that would help.

"You look preoccupied. How did your implantation go today?"

I looked up. Ruth, my partner, was standing in the doorway. She came into my office and shut the door behind her.

"I think it went well, but we'll obviously have to wait to see if it took," I said.

Apart from Daniel, and my best friend Andrea, Ruth was the only other person in whom I had confided. I didn't want any questions, or any sympathy, if my efforts failed. Ruth would deliver me if I was successful, and after all our years practicing together, I knew I could trust her discretion.

"Is anything else on your mind?" she asked.

She plopped down on my patient chair, kicked off her shoes and put her feet, in their sheer black tights, on my desk.

"Apart from someone wanting to bomb our office, I just had a particularly narcissistic patient. Louise did her in vitro fertilization, and she was complaining about how inconvenient it was that Louise died."

"Some things can't be cured," Ruth said. "Go home and eat something fattening."

"Easy for you to say."

Ruth was five-foot-ten, had the build of a ballerina, and was the fashion maven in our office. I still remember the day I met her during our residency. I was wearing scrubs that had been slept in, and Ruth was writing a note at the nurses' station, wearing a gorgeous red cashmere sweater. We'd been in practice together for ten years now, and I swear she never gained an ounce.

"I'm still so upset about Louise. Even ice cream won't make that better."

I wanted so badly to discuss Louise with someone else who knew her, but I couldn't breach the confidentiality of Daniel's case. If he had wanted our office to know about Louise going undercover, he would have said something.

Ruth removed her feet from my desk, leaned forward, and reached for my hand.

"I know," she said. "She was a colleague to both of us, and one of your doctors. I know how horrified I am. I can only imagine what you're experiencing."

"Did you know her well? I mean, on a personal level?"

"Not really. She was quite a bit older than I am. We didn't move in the same circles. She was mainly someone I referred patients to for infertility."

Ruth had just given me an idea. It would be easy enough to research Louise's background and see if any of the older doctors on our medical staff knew her during college or residency. I'd do that tomorrow. Right now, I just wanted to go home to my family and maybe eat something fattening after all.

CHAPTER TWENTY-FOUR

Daniel pulled his car into the garage, took a few deep breaths to wind down, and opened the door into the kitchen.

"Daniel, you're home early!" Zoe ran down the hall toward him and he scooped her up in his arms for a hug.

"Hey Princess, what are you up to?" His frustration at having to wait all afternoon for news from the FBI faded. Zoe always had that effect on him. She was better than a blood pressure pill.

"I'm playing a race car driver video game Mommy bought me on the TV. Want to play it with me?"

"Absolutely." It may have been a mistake for Hannah to take her to the Peterson Museum. Pretty soon, she'd be asking for a flight simulator.

"Mom home?" he asked.

"Not yet, but Emilia made us dinner."

"Hey, Emilia," Daniel said, peeking into the kitchen. "Something smells great."

"Chicken enchiladas and guacamole, Mr. Daniel."

Emilia was a fabulous cook. She was only five-foot-two

and weighed in at over two-hundred pounds, with a round face, dark almond eyes and jet black hair. She was in her fifties and had raised three children on her own, after divorcing their father.

"My favorite. Thank you. You can head home now, if you like."

Her generous mouth flashed him a big smile. Emilia gave the kitchen counter one more swipe with a sponge, retrieved her purse, and hugged Zoe on her way out.

Daniel returned to the den. He sat down in front of the TV and waited, while Zoe raced her Lamborghini around the track.

"See if you can beat my time," she said.

Daniel chose a bright yellow Porsche and clicked GO. Just then, his cell phone rang. It was FBI Agent Brian Anderson.

"Do you have to answer that? You're gonna lose."

"Afraid so, sweetie. Give me five minutes."

He stood up and answered the call.

"This is Detective Ross," he said, walking out of Zoe's hearing range.

"Thought I'd share the good news," Anderson said. "Our SWAT team arrested all three guys at the ranch, and confiscated a large supply of weapons and bomb-making equipment, plus a few bombs ready to go. We've got them locked in interrogation rooms."

"Did you find Karl Schmidt and his daughter?" Daniel asked.

"That didn't require a SWAT team," Anderson said. "We'll be questioning the men tonight. We won't mention your murder. We can do the Schmidts together, in the morning."

"Much appreciated. I'll be there early. You made my day."

"Can you play now?" Zoe asked.

"I think it's your turn again," Daniel said, as he ended the call and settled back down on the sofa. "Let's do this before your mother gets back."

About half-an-hour later, Daniel heard Hannah's footsteps in the front hall.

"I see the new video game is a hit," Hannah said, putting down her purse, and peering over their shoulders at the TV screen.

"Hi, love. How was your afternoon?" Daniel said.

She shrugged and kissed the top of Zoe's head.

"Hi, Mommy, want to play?"

"Why don't you finish beating Daniel, while I go warm up supper?"

Zoe turned her attention back to the screen.

"I got an interesting new patient this afternoon," Hannah said. "Her husband is the plaintiff in that lawsuit I discovered the other day."

"No kidding," Daniel said, his attention wandering from his Porsche.

"Have you interviewed the husband yet?" Hannah asked.

"I won, Daniel," Zoe announced.

Daniel sighed. "You always win, Princess."

"That's because you don't pay attention," Zoe said.

After dinner, with Zoe in her room doing her homework, Daniel updated Hannah on the case.

"Do you think you can get one of those guys to admit to killing Louise?" Hannah asked.

"The security footage says they didn't. We were able to trace all their cars to the freeway on-ramp. But, maybe they know who did. In the meantime, all suspects are still in the running. I'm not ruling out one of her partners, or someone from her past that we know nothing about. She may have had more of a secret life than just being undercover at the FPA."

"Have you ever gone undercover?" Hannah asked. "It seems like such a scary thing to do."

"Just once, when I first joined the LAPD. I was working the narcotics division. I used to go out, dressed like a junkie, and try to score some coke or heroin. Then, my backups would arrest the dealers. It wasn't fun, but it was a lot less dangerous than what Louise was doing."

"I've been invited to a dinner tomorrow night, hosted by Westside Fertility Associates, something to do with surrogacy. Louise's partners will be there, and if they're still suspects, perhaps I should go. You never know what I might overhear."

"Good idea."

Hannah couldn't get into any trouble at some expensive Beverly Hills restaurant, and she had a genius for acquiring useful information. At least she was checking with him before she went off investigating on her own. He didn't want her taking any risks, especially if she was pregnant.

He slipped his arms around her and kissed her neck. "So where is this event?" he asked.

"Spago," she said. "It'll be tough eating that food, but someone's got to do it."

CHAPTER TWENTY-FIVE

I WOKE UP AT 6:30 A.M. AND TREATED myself to a long, hot shower. Daniel joined me in the middle of it, which made the shower even longer, and improved my mood considerably. I chose a chic black suit, suitable for tonight's dinner, and took some extra time taming my curly red hair.

Even with all the extras, I managed to get to my office an hour early, emailed a belated RSVP to Westside Fertility Associates, and sat at my computer to do some sleuthing. The information I wanted was not hard to retrieve.

Louise's resume was on the practice website. She'd been an undergraduate at Berkeley, then went to UCLA Medical School, did her Ob-Gyn Residency at NYU, and had an endocrine fellowship at UC San Francisco. I jotted down the dates and places. Then I turned my attention to the Memorial Hospital physician list.

Every member of my department was listed, along with the date each had joined the hospital staff. Once again, resumes were easy to find, and I made note of anyone who might have crossed paths with Louise during her younger days. Of the physicians I investigated, two, including her partner, Ian Price, had graduated UCLA. It would be nice if both potential suspects were at Spago tonight. I recalled Frances Conners mentioning Louise's activities in college, during the Planned Parenthood fundraiser. Frances wasn't on staff at Memorial, but a quick Google check revealed that she had been at Berkeley. That seemed a good place to start.

I picked up the phone, called Planned Parenthood, and was told she was operating. I left a message. Enough sleuthing for now. It was Daniel's turn.

CHAPTER TWENTY-SIX

D ANIEL ARRIVED EARLY AT FBI headquarters and was escorted to Brian Anderson's cramped office, where both Agent Anderson and Agent Russo awaited him.

"Any luck with the interviews?" Daniel asked.

Anderson smiled. "We've got our three little bomb makers in separate rooms, and each one is trying to blame the others, and cut a deal with us to be a witness."

"No honor among thieves and terrorists," Daniel said. "What do they say about Karl and Karen-Kay Schmidt?"

"We're getting the same story from each of them, so it's probably true. They claim they're hired guns, not at all interested in the anti-abortion movement, and that Karl contacted them about three months ago to provide the explosives. They were being well paid."

"Did you ask them what they knew about Karen-Kay and Mildred?"

"They all claim to have met the women for the first time Thursday night. Other than that, they know nothing."

"What have you gotten out of Karl Schmidt and his daughter, so far?" Daniel asked.

"Nothing. It was quite late by the time we arrested them, so we read them their rights and parked them in cells. Then we had to transfer them here from Orange County. Neither of them have asked for a lawyer yet, so we'd better interview them before they change their minds."

"I wonder why they didn't ask," Daniel said.

"Stupidity or arrogance. Schmidt probably thinks he's smarter than we are. Let's not look a gift horse in the mouth. I suggest we start with her. Why don't you take Agent Russo in with you? Karen-Kay might be more talkative if there's another woman in the room."

"Sounds like a plan," Daniel said.

Karen-Kay Schmidt was seated at the table in the interrogation room. Her shoulders were hunched, her head, with its uncombed, mousy-brown hair, was down, and her hands were clenched in her lap. She raised her eyes as they entered. They were red and swollen, with dark circles below them. She obviously hadn't gotten any sleep.

Agent Russo placed a recording device on the table and introduced herself.

"I'm FBI Agent Isobel Russo and this is LAPD Detective Daniel Ross. We'd like to ask you a few questions. We read you your rights last night, but I'm going to repeat them for the recording." She switched on the device and proceeded.

"This recording is being made at the FBI field office in West Los Angeles. Agent Isobel Russo and Detective Daniel Ross are present, interviewing Karen-Kay Schmidt." Russo repeated the Miranda rights.

Karen-Kay finally raised her head. "Why am I here and where is my father?"

"You, Miss Schmidt, are here because we have evidence that you are part of a terrorist plot to blow up facilities that perform abortions," Russo said.

"That's not true," Karen-Kay said. "I would never do such a thing."

Russo shook her head. "Planning to murder innocent doctors and patients will send you to prison for a very long time. If anyone is killed, you'll be there for life. Have you already planted one of those bombs?"

"No, I would never kill anyone."

"We have witnesses who say otherwise."

"What witnesses?"

"Three men who say your father hired them to make bombs for you to place in offices that perform abortions. They're all willing to testify in court, and we've confiscated the bombs."

"My father is a man of God," Karen-Kay said. "He believes in defending innocent lives. Why aren't you arresting those doctors who murder defenseless fetuses?"

Russo glanced at Daniel and he leaned forward, placing his arms on the table.

"So, your father was planning to kill doctors and patients to defend innocent fetuses?" Daniel asked.

"No, no one was supposed to get killed. We just wanted to send a message by blowing up the facilities when no one was there."

"I see. Would you like to explain how those bombs were going to be put in place?"

"Mildred was going to do it."

Daniel sat back and waited until she met his eyes. "Tell us about Mildred. How long was she a part of your group?"

"She joined us a few months ago. She's very passionate about our cause. Her sister died years ago from a botched abortion. She was willing to do anything."

"How did Mildred find you?"

"We have a website and a chat room. My father uses it to

recruit our most loyal supporters and will occasionally invite them to our private meetings."

"Do you happen to have a last name and an address for Mildred?"

"We don't share that information."

"So how do you communicate with your new recruits?"

"My Dad's a preacher. He invites people to church through the chat room, meets them, and decides if they're trustworthy. If he plans to invite someone to a particular meeting, he gives them a throw-away phone and calls them with the time and address."

"Very clever. So what, exactly, was this Mildred planning to do?"

"She was going to make an appointment in an office that did abortions, plant a bomb, and set it off at night, after the office closed."

"And what office did she choose?" Russo asked.

"She wasn't supposed to tell us. We would find out when the bombing made the news."

"Do you know if she made that appointment and placed the bomb?"

"I have no idea."

"You, yourself, were not planning to also make an appointment and bomb an office?"

"No. My daddy didn't want me to do anything dangerous."

"When was the last time you saw Mildred?" Daniel asked.

"Thursday night. She was at our meeting."

"Are you referring to the meeting at the storefront on Pico Boulevard?"

"Yes."

"Did you leave together?"

"No. Mildred left first. Daddy and I left about fifteen minutes later."

"Where did you go when you left the meeting?"

"We drove straight home to Anaheim," Karen-Kay said.

"You didn't follow Mildred home?" Daniel asked.

"No, why would we?"

"How do you plan to get in touch with her when the bombs are ready?"

"I told you. My daddy gave her a phone."

Now it was Russo's turn to lean forward and force Karen-Kay to look at her.

"You know, you are in a world of trouble," Russo said. "Even if you didn't personally plant a bomb, you're still going to prison for conspiracy. We might be able to cut you a deal if you agree to testify against Mildred."

Karen-Kay chewed on her lower lip. "I don't know. I think maybe I should talk to a lawyer."

"Do you have one you want to call?" Russo asked.

"No."

"We'll notify the public defender's office. Interview terminated at nine-fourteen a.m."

After Karen-Kay was escorted back to her cell, Daniel, Russo and Anderson reconvened in Anderson's office.

"What do you think?" Anderson asked.

"I think she's an accomplished little liar," Russo said. "We know from the recording that both of the women were supposed to place bombs. She was all too ready to place the blame on Mildred, and I wouldn't be surprised if Daddy backs up her story."

"Yeah, but she did refer to Mildred in the present tense. I

think she really doesn't know that Mildred is Louise, and Louise is dead. Let's see if she agrees to testify, and let's see if Daddy will give us the phone number," Daniel said.

"Did you guys find that phone?" Russo asked.

"Unfortunately, no. We found her personal iPhone under the seat in her car, but we haven't located her purse or the burner phone."

"Well, shall we see if we can get Daddy to cooperate?" Anderson asked.

Unlike his daughter, who appeared tearful and frightened, Karl Schmidt sat straight with a scowl on his face. After the preliminaries were complete, Schmidt asked, "Why the hell am I here?"

"You," Anderson said, "are being accused of master-minding a plot to place bombs in the offices of doctors who perform abortions."

"That's absurd. You can't prove any of that."

"We just arrested three men who will swear, independently, in court, that you hired them to make the bombs. We have also confiscated the bombs."

"They're lying," Schmidt shouted.

"We also have video from surveillance cameras showing that you and these men met at a storefront on Pico Boulevard Thursday night, along with your daughter and another woman. Do you deny that meeting?"

Schmidt said nothing.

Daniel stared at Schmidt. "We've interviewed your daughter, Karen-Kay. Were you planning to have her and Mildred pose as patients and hide the bombs?"

"You leave Karen-Kay out of this."

"Are you suggesting Karen-Kay wasn't going to bomb a doctor's office and kill innocent patients? Your daughter is in deep trouble. She's going to jail for a very long time."

"You can't put us in jail for something that never happened," Schmidt said. "You hear about any bombs going off?"

"It's called conspiracy," Daniel said. "Tell us about Mildred. We want to know where she is. We know you gave her a burner phone."

"I haven't heard from her."

"You try calling her?"

Schmidt nodded.

"Was that a yes?" Anderson asked.

"Yes."

Daniel glanced over at Anderson. Schmidt's phone would be checked.

"How many times did you call her?" Daniel asked.

Schmidt shrugged. "Two, maybe three times."

"You leave a message?" Anderson asked.

"No need. She'd know who to call. I was the only one with the number."

Daniel waited a while to frame his next question. "It turns out Mildred isn't going to be able to call you back. Her body was found on Friday, in a dumpster near the 10 Freeway. Did you kill her?"

Schmidt looked stunned, but Daniel thought maybe he was just a good actor.

"You're bullshitting me. I don't believe you."

"It's true."

"Why would I want to kill her? And why would I call her, if I knew she was dead?"

"You'd call her to make us believe you didn't know she

was dead. What happened? Did you decide you couldn't trust her? Is that why you killed her?"

"No. I had nothing to do with that."

"When was the last time you saw her?"

"Thursday night. She left our meeting, and then Karen-Kay and I drove home."

"Did you hire someone to kill her after the meeting?" Daniel asked.

"I think I'll take that lawyer now," Schmidt said.

"Very well. We'll have more questions later. We'll notify your lawyer of the date and time of your arraignment." Anderson turned off the recording device, and he and Daniel left the room.

"We'll trace the call and see if we can locate that burner phone for you," Anderson said.

"Thanks," Daniel said. "I'm heading back to the office. I'm hoping the forensics and autopsy report will be ready. I'll keep you posted."

CHAPTER TWENTY-SEVEN

"Hᴏᴡ'ᴅ ɪᴛ ɢᴏ?" Bʀᴇɴᴅᴀ ʟᴏᴏᴋᴇᴅ ᴜᴘ from her desk as Daniel entered the detectives' squad room.

"So-so. We shouldn't have any trouble convicting them all of conspiracy, but we're no closer to nailing any of them for Louise's murder."

"Too bad you can't use that video recording in court," Brenda said.

"Inadmissible without Louise on the stand to back it up."

"It seems as if Louise must have been grabbed just as she got to her car. Her keys were on the floor, and she had obviously just put the water bottle in the beverage holder, but her purse wasn't there."

Daniel tried to visualize the scene. It made sense. "The question is, where did he take her, and can we tie him to the FPA?"

Brenda reached into her top drawer and pulled out a manila envelope. "The forensics are back from the storefront and from her car. They're not helpful. Bill Pincus called. The autopsy is done. You might want to talk to him before you read these."

"Thanks." Daniel took the envelope to his desk, and picked up the phone to call the County Coroner's office.

"What have you got for me, Bill?"

"The cause of death was strangulation by hand. It's the sort of death I associate with a very angry killer who wants to get up close and personal. She was tied up and tortured before he killed her. There are traces of hemp from rope on her T shirt. The killer used duct tape on both wrists and to tie her ankles together. I found bruises on her chest and abdomen, and a fracture on her jaw. Most of the face was gone, because of the rats."

Daniel winced. There was no way he was going to share any of those details with Hannah. "Anything else?" he asked.

"One more surprise. She was dying. I found metastatic pancreatic cancer all over her abdominal cavity and liver. If she hadn't been murdered, I doubt she'd have lasted another month."

"Do you think she knew?" Daniel asked.

"Hard to say. Pancreatic cancer can be asymptomatic for a long time, and then the symptoms are nausea, weight loss, and lack of appetite. Abdominal pain starts later. You know how doctors are. They have a habit of ignoring their own symptoms and treating themselves."

"If she knew, maybe that explains why she was willing to take such a big risk," Daniel said. "I'm going to have to talk to her husband again. Thanks."

Brenda was staring at him from across her desk. Daniel filled her in.

"If the FPA wanted to get rid of her, and sent someone to ambush her, why not just shoot or stab her and leave the body in the car? Why the torture?"

"Maybe they wanted to know who she was working for and who she had told," Daniel said.

"If that was the case," Brenda went on, "once they found out, why didn't they get rid of the evidence? Why sit there with a bunch of bombs and wait to be arrested five days later?"

"Good point," Daniel said. He leaned back in his chair and opened the manila envelope.

The storefront was a treasure trove of prints and DNA. The lab had been able to identify all three skinheads as well as the Schmidts. There was no trace evidence or blood suggesting that Louise had been tortured there. Daniel sighed and put the forensic report back in his desk.

"I think you and I should pay a visit to Hank Waldman," he said. "The coroner is ready to release Louise's body and I have some questions for him."

Daniel called Waldman on his cell. He said he was at his office.

"Working is the only way I can take my mind off this, even if only for a few minutes at a time."

"We have some new information for you and a few more questions. Can we meet?"

Hank told them to come to his office at two in the afternoon, so Daniel took Brenda to a local sushi restaurant for lunch. He needed a break from the station.

The office of Astrodyne Engineering and Technology was in an industrial park on Ocean Avenue in Santa Monica.

"What does Hank Waldman do?" Brenda asked.

"His firm designs rocket parts for NASA," Daniel said. "Hank's got a PhD in aeronautical engineering from MIT, and an MBA from USC."

"Smart guy," she said.

The company occupied two floors of a four-story building, and the office had a very utilitarian look. No fancy artwork or designer chairs. This was a place where scientists retreated to their small offices and created spaceships. Daniel approved.

A middle-aged receptionist wearing wire rim glasses greeted them, had them sign in, and issued badges. A security guard escorted them back to Hank Waldman's office. It was a modest-sized room, the walls adorned with photographs from the Hubble Space telescope. Hank got up from his desk, shook their hands, and motioned them toward two chairs.

In the interval since they first met him, he seemed to have aged ten years. His face was gaunt, his eyes haunted, his hair unwashed. He looked like he hadn't slept in days.

"Have you found out who killed her?" he asked.

"Not yet," Daniel said. "But we've learned a great deal about what she was doing. Were you aware that Louise was attending meetings of a right-wing anti-abortion group, undercover?"

"I had no idea. If I'd known, I'd have attempted to stop her. But I'm not surprised. Louise was an adventuress and she had a frightening disregard for her own safety. The riskier it was, the more she liked doing it."

"We found a hidden camera in her car," Daniel said. "Thanks to her recording, we were able to arrest the cell and confiscate the bombs they were planning to plant in the offices of doctors who do abortions."

"Do you think those people killed her?" Hank asked.

"We did, initially, but we haven't been able to tie any of them directly to her murder."

"It's possible that they hired someone to lay in wait for her," Brenda said. "But it's also possible that her death had nothing to do with her undercover work."

"How did she die?" Hank asked.

"She was strangled," Daniel answered. "But the autopsy also revealed that she had metastatic pancreatic cancer."

There was a sharp intake of breath as Hank clenched his fists.

"Was she aware of her diagnosis? Were you?"

Hank put his head in his hands and silently stared down at his desk. When he finally looked up, his eyes were wet. "She only found out a few weeks ago. They suggested chemotherapy, but she knew enough to realize that it wouldn't make a difference. She might gain a month or two, at the cost of feeling incredibly sick the whole time. We talked it over. She just wanted to live her normal life for as long as she could, and when she couldn't, she would go into hospice care. We didn't even tell George. She didn't want to disrupt his freshman year at college until it was absolutely necessary."

"She must have been a very brave woman," Brenda said.

"The bastard who killed her robbed me of our last few months together," Hank said, his voice breaking. "You have to find him."

"We're following every possible lead," Daniel said. "That's why we wanted to talk to you. Can you think of anyone, perhaps from Louise's adventurous past, who might have hated her? What kind of risky things did she do?"

"When I met Louise, she had just begun her infertility practice, and I was a junior scientist at JPL. She loved the outdoors and was an accomplished technical climber. She also enjoyed recreational parachuting. The biggest argument we ever had occurred after George was born, and I insisted she stop jumping out of airplanes because I didn't want to wind up a single father."

"Did she stop?"

"Under protest. She found a substitute in exotic travel. Every year, she'd go on some two week medical mission to the ends of the earth, often in war zones or places where terrorists were common. She'd do pap smears in refugee camps in the Sudan, or go to Nigeria to fix fistulas for women who'd had a traumatic childbirth. It made her feel like she was making a difference, but I also think she got off on the danger. But to answer your first question, I can't think of anyone who hated her enough to kill her. "

"Did she like to experiment with drugs?" Brenda asked.

"Not when I knew her, but I know she was pretty wild in her Berkeley days. That was before my time. You'd have to talk to one of her old friends."

"Can you give us a name?" Daniel asked.

"Her closest friend was Frances Conners. They were roommates at Berkeley. Frances runs Planned Parenthood in Los Angeles."

"What about the men in her life? Is there an angry ex-boyfriend out there somewhere?"

"I don't know," Hank said. "We'd both had a number of romantic relationships before we married, and we decided that they weren't worth discussing. We were married twenty-five years, so all of that would be ancient history."

"Thank you, Mr. Waldman," Daniel said. "The coroner is ready to release Louise's body, so you can plan the funeral. I would like to ask you not to release any photos of her to the news media. I don't want anyone from the anti-abortion group to make the connection between Louise and the woman they knew as Mildred. There may be more of them out there."

"I understand. Thank you."

Daniel and Brenda left the office and returned to their car.

"What now, boss?" Brenda asked. "You want to look up Frances Conners?"

"Frances Conners is the source of the FPA information that Hannah uncovered," Daniel said. "Hannah knows her quite well. I think I'll see if she can extract some additional information before we get into the act. It will give her something safe to do, and she can probably get Frances talking better than we can. I'll ask her when she gets home tonight. She's dining at Spago."

CHAPTER TWENTY-EIGHT

I HANDED MY CAR KEY TO THE PARKING valet, and headed for the bar where waiters were circulating with glasses of wine and exotic variations on pizza. The seminar was going to be well attended. I had already spotted quite a few colleagues.

Ian Price, one of Louise's two partners, was holding court in the center of the room, in conversation with Myron Rabinowitz, one of the UCLA medical school alumni I wanted to find. I grabbed a Sauvignon Blanc and drifted over to them. I'd known Myron since my internship and he'd always been a kind mentor. He leaned over and kissed my cheek. His bright blue eyes twinkled, a sharp contrast to his gray hair and beard.

"How are you, my dear," he said.

"Still in shock over Louise," I answered. "You both went to medical school with her?"

"We did," Ian said. "But she was three years ahead of me. I didn't get to know her until I was an endocrine fellow at Memorial."

"Were you in her class?" I asked Myron.

"I graduated before she got there," he said. "Such a tragedy."

So much for my investigation into Louise's past. Ian excused himself and moved on, shaking hands as he went. I spotted Kaspar Nazari, Louise's other partner, doing the same, at the other end of the bar.

"It should be an interesting evening. Surrogacy is such a controversial topic," Myron said. "When I went into practice it was inconceivable that one woman could pay another to have her baby. I still find the idea disquieting. Have you ever delivered a surrogate?"

"Not so far," I said. As an intern, I had assisted on a caesarian section for a young woman who had served as both surrogate and egg donor. Her unexpected death was my first introduction to murder, and not something I wanted to remember or talk about. "I worry that the practice is so unregulated. It's ripe for exploitation of poor women by wealthy ones."

"I can see that," Myron said. "I can also imagine that, because they need the money, women who are unsuitable to be surrogates volunteer."

"Unsuitable for what reasons?" I asked.

"Medical reasons. Not everyone can have an uncomplicated pregnancy."

"True. Unfortunately, doctors don't select the surrogates," I said. "I'm sure, like everything else now, patients just go online. I wouldn't be surprised if there was an app, like e-Harmony, for surrogates, but patients don't have the medical knowledge to ask the right questions."

"Then, there's the fact that surrogacy is becoming a big international business," Myron added. "They can ship embryos anywhere."

"I didn't know that," I said.

"It will be interesting to hear what the speaker has to say. I think we are about to go into the private dining room for dinner." He took my arm. "Will you join me?"

CHAPTER TWENTY-NINE

W HEN MYRON AND I TOOK OUR SEATS, Nori Tanaka
slid into the chair beside me.

"How are you?" she whispered.

"So far, so good," I said.

The waiter served the heirloom tomato salad and offered another glass of Sauvignon Blanc. I declined.

Kaspar Nazari rose from his seat and walked to the podium.

"Ladies and gentlemen, thank you for coming. Our topic for this evening is surrogacy. How can you help your patient select the right surrogate for her baby? Our speaker is Miss Courtney Duchamps, the founder and CEO of Beverly Hills Surrogacy Institute."

Miss Duchamps rose and acknowledged the applause. We all returned to our tomatoes as she began speaking. There was something about her appearance that I found off-putting. Duchamps sounded like the stage name of an actress. She was tall and wearing a very unprofessional bright blue, jersey spandex dress, that clung to every prominence and revealed a subtle glimpse of cleavage. Any lower, and her neckline would have been appropriate for the Oscars. Her pretty face was nipped, tucked, professionally made up, and went well with her abundant blonde waves. It wasn't very tolerant of me, but I took an instant dislike to her.

"So thrilled to be here with all you wonderful doctors," Courtney began. She used her remote control to dim the lights and begin a Power Point presentation. "We are a full service agency. Not only do we recruit healthy surrogates for you, but we arrange for their medical records to be available and for all the important laboratory tests to be done."

A slide showed a list of sexually transmitted diseases, as well as basic screening tests for diabetes and heart disease. This was followed by photos of remarkably attractive pregnant surrogates and happy parents. The women could have all gotten jobs as models.

"We also provide complete legal services for both the gestational carrier and the intended parents," she continued. "As you may be aware, the legal situation with respect to surrogacy is still in flux, so careful legal consultation is critical to protect all parties. I will be passing around our brochures, and my card, so that any of you who need surrogacy services in your practices know how to reach us. Does anyone have any questions before the main course is served?"

Myron raised a hand. "Where and how do you recruit your surrogates?"

"Most of them come to us through our website. We then collect some basic information, and if the woman seems as if she might qualify, we interview her in person."

I raised my hand "What does it cost?"

Courtney gave a coy smile. "Well, the couple is expected to pick up all medical expenses, as well as an agency fee and a legal fee for their attorney. There is also, of course, some compensation for the surrogate."

The busboy removed the salad plates, and a waiter replaced mine with a plate of Jidori chicken with wild mushrooms, goat cheese, and Yukon Gold potato purée. I took a bite and decided it was worth listening to Courtney just for the dinner.

Myron leaned toward me. "What's your impression of Courtney?"

I rolled my eyes. "She doesn't inspire my trust." I turned to Nori. "Do you happen to know where the ladies room is?"

"I'll come with you," she said.

I was hoping she'd offer. The ladies room was usually an excellent place for a private conversation. As we were washing our hands at adjacent sinks, and reapplying our makeup, I asked "What do you know about this Surrogacy Institute? Are they legitimate?"

Nori shrugged. "Ian and Kaspar have been putting this deal together for the past few months. I wasn't asked to participate and Louise didn't want anything to do with it."

"Why not? Was there some financial connection between your practice and the surrogacy institute? If there is anything I know about Louise, it's that she was the kind of doctor who would avoid conflicts of interest."

"I don't know," Nori said.

"Did Louise argue with Ian and Kaspar about it?" I was on the alert now.

"Not while I was listening."

"Why didn't they offer to include you?"

"I'm just the new hire, not a partner yet. No one tells me anything." She didn't sound very happy about it. "I don't know if they will even keep me on when the dust settles.

Louise hired me and neither of the men has been particularly friendly."

"I'd be sorry to hear that Nori, but if you part ways with them, you can count on me to send you patients, wherever you practice."

She turned toward me with a half-hearted smile. "Thank you, Hannah, that means a great deal."

At that moment, two giggling millennials entered the bathroom, putting an end to any private conversation, and we returned to the dinner table.

I scooped up a forkful of Yukon gold potatoes and decided this conversation might be worth mentioning to Daniel.

It was shortly after nine when I got home. Zoe was already asleep, and Daniel was on the sofa in the den, absorbed in his laptop.

"Working?" I asked.

He looked up at me and closed the computer. "Just reviewing all the security footage again. I was hoping I'd missed something critical. So far, no luck. How was dinner?"

"The food was great, and the talk was provocative. Apparently, Kaspar Nazari and Ian Price have formed a business relationship with the Beverly Hills Surrogacy Institute, run by a woman named Courtney Duchamps. Nori said that Louise disapproved. I thought you should know."

"Are you saying there was some conflict about it within the practice?"

"Sounds like it," I said. "I thought it might be worth your while to do a background check on Miss Duchamps and her

Institute. There was something about her that raised my hackles."

"I've always trusted your hackles," Daniel laughed.

"Is it illegal for a fertility practice to have a financial relationship with a surrogacy agency?" Hannah asked.

"I guess that depends on the relationship. Kickbacks for referrals would certainly be illegal."

"Not to mention, unethical. One thing I know about Louise is that her ethics were above reproach. If she didn't want anything to do with this, there was a good reason."

Daniel got up from the sofa and began massaging my shoulders.

I relaxed into his chest.

"Thanks for the suggestion. I'll ask Izzy to see what he can find tomorrow. By the way, I have a job for you. Hank Waldman said that Frances Conners was Louise's best friend. Could you talk to her again, and see what you can dig up about Louise's past romantic life?"

"Sure. What are you thinking?"

"I'm wondering if there were any angry ex-boyfriends who might have reappeared. Hank claims to know nothing. It may be a reach, but it's a loose end I'd like to tie up, and I suspect Frances will be more forthcoming with you than with me."

"It just so happens that Frances and I have a lunch date tomorrow," I said.

Daniel completed my shoulder massage and turned me toward him, tipping my chin up for a kiss. "That's my girl. Always ten steps ahead of me."

CHAPTER THIRTY

"WHY SO GLUM?" BRENDA SAID, AS Daniel walked into the office the next morning.

"I feel like a bloodhound who's lost the scent, and is running around in circles, trying to pick it up again," Daniel said.

Brenda reached for her coffee and took another sip. "I get it."

"I'll never forgive myself if we don't solve this case."

"You worried that Hannah will be disappointed in you?"

"She won't have to be. I'll be upset enough with me for the both of us."

Izzy peered at the two of them over the top of his computer screen. "Does that mean you've run out of things for me to do?"

"Actually not," Daniel said. "Hannah mentioned something she heard last night that might be worth following up on. Can you check out the ownership and financials on something called Beverly Hills Surrogacy Institute? The CEO is a woman named Courtney Duchamps. Apparently, there was a sharp difference of opinion between Louise and her two partners about getting involved with them."

"Sounds as if we should take a closer look at the two partners," Brenda said. "We dropped that ball initially, when it appeared that neither one had anything to gain financially from Louise's death. But, as I recall, neither of them had an alibi we could confirm either."

"Right," said Daniel. "Both of them said they were home all night, Price alone, and Nazari with his wife, who would no doubt confirm anything he wanted her to say."

Daniel's cell phone rang. "FBI," he said, glancing at the screen.

"While you take that call," Brenda said, "I'll check out Miss Duchamps. Maybe she has a record."

As Daniel answered the phone, Brenda turned to her computer. She looked up with a grin, a few minutes later, as Daniel finished his call and walked over to her desk.

"What news from the Feds?" she asked.

Daniel sat down opposite her. "That was Anderson. They've been tracing all the calls made from Schmidt's burner phone, as well as his regular cell, hoping to track down more members of the FPA. The calls to Louise's phone all went from Anaheim to the same cell tower in Mid-Wilshire."

"Did they try calling from some other locations, to see if they could triangulate the location of the phone?"

"They tried, but it had clearly run out of battery power, so nothing went through. It does seem likely that the purse and the phone haven't moved since Louise was captured and killed. Unfortunately, it's a large radius. We did a dumpster check on all the streets close to the body and the car last Friday, and came up blank," Daniel said.

"Maybe the phone wasn't tossed out. What if the killer

tortured her at a house not far from the dump site and her purse is still there?" Brenda suggested.

"I don't think any judge would give us a warrant to search every home in a mile radius," Daniel said.

"Oh, well, this should cheer you up. Courtney Duchamps has a record. She ran an escort service in West Hollywood for years. Maybe that's why the surrogates on her website are so hot looking."

Daniel's jaw dropped. "Seriously?" He was beginning to think that Hannah was a witch.

Brenda leaned over and fluttered her eyelashes at him. "Sweetheart, don't you think it's time you and I gave up trying to make me pregnant, and made an appointment to hire a surrogate?"

"Let's see if we can get an appointment for tomorrow morning."

"We're in at ten a.m.," Brenda said, a few minutes later.

"Well done. Can you come over tonight? I think Hannah should brief us on our cover story, so we get the medical details right."

"I'll be there right after dinner."

CHAPTER THIRTY-ONE

I scheduled myself for a two-hour lunch, so that Frances Conners and I would have plenty of time to talk. Frances was waiting when I got to Langer's Deli and we snagged a comfortable booth near the rear of the restaurant. We decided to split a pastrami sandwich and both of us ordered Doctor Brown's cream soda. I reached for a sour pickle with a sigh of contentment.

"So, have you heard any news about the investigation into Louise's murder?" Frances asked.

"Daniel's in charge," I said. "He asked me to talk to you. He thinks you might have helpful information."

"About what?"

"They're following several trails. One concerns Louise's past. As you told me, she was quite a risk taker. He wanted to know if you could think of any ex-boyfriend with a grudge."

The waiter arrived with the food and an extra plate. We divided the gigantic sandwich. I added hot sweet mustard and some cole slaw, and took a large bite.

"Divine," I said.

The waiter was no longer within earshot. I waited for Frances to sample her food.

"Louise cut quite a swath among the young men at Berkeley. Frankly, she slept around and thoroughly enjoyed herself. It was mostly one- or two-night stands. Louise was serious about her studies and didn't have time for a long-term relationship."

"Wasn't there anyone who lasted longer than one night?" I asked.

"There was one guy, senior year, whom she dated consistently. As I recall, he was a gorgeous hunk and very athletic. They were always going backpacking, snowboarding, parasailing and rock climbing."

"It exhausts me just thinking about it. How long did it last?"

"They broke up toward the end of senior year. As I recall, it wasn't pleasant. Louise was in a foul mood and wouldn't tell me why she ended it," Frances said.

"Was she the one who dumped him?" I asked.

"I think so. He hung around our apartment for a while afterwards, but she refused to see him."

"Then what?"

"Then she went to medical school, and as far as I know, they never saw one another again," Frances said.

"Do you remember his name?"

"I'm afraid not. It was thirty years ago. Why didn't Daniel just come and ask me these questions himself?"

"He's trying to give me something useful to do, so I won't go charging off, investigating on my own. He asks me to do things that he deems safe."

"Don't you find that a bit patronizing?"

"I would if it were anyone else. Unfortunately, when I investigated some of his other cases, I managed to get into trouble, although I must add that my snooping was very successful. So, Daniel's gotten a bit overprotective. But, I saw how frightened and upset he was getting, and frankly, I don't like being in danger."

"I see."

"By the way, you don't happen to still have your Berkeley class yearbook? Maybe, if we look through it, you might recognize the boyfriend?"

"I'm sure I do have it, the only question is where? If you buy me cheesecake for dessert, I'll look for it when I get home."

"It's a deal," I said.

I arrived home shortly after Daniel, with a large assortment of desserts from Langer's. After all, if Brenda was coming over this evening, I had to be a good hostess. She rang the bell shortly after 7:30 p.m., and Zoe ran for the door.

"Hi, kiddo," Brenda said. "What's up with you?"

Zoe thought for a moment. "I might want to be a detective like you when I grow up," she announced.

"Not a doctor like your mom?"

"Mom has to get up in the middle of the night all the time," Zoe said. "She should have been an eye doctor."

"I'll take that under advisement. In my next life, maybe I'll do an ophthalmology residency." I turned to Brenda. "I've got dessert."

"Anything chocolate?" Brenda asked. "I concentrate so much better on chocolate."

"Me too," said Zoe.

"Brownies for both of you. Zoe, why don't you take your dessert and a glass of milk into the den?"

"Why, Mommy?"

"Because I have to teach Daniel and Brenda all about medicine. You'll be bored."

Zoe complied, and I poured decaf for the three of us in the kitchen. "So, how can I help?"

"We're going undercover to the Surrogacy Institute tomorrow, to consult them about hiring a surrogate," Brenda explained. "What reason could I give for wanting to do that?"

I thought about it. "You have breast cancer," I said. "You've had surgery and are finishing up your radiation therapy. You'll be done in a few weeks, and then you start a drug which will stop you from making estrogen. Your doctor says that it's too dangerous for you to get pregnant. The high estrogen levels during pregnancy will cause the tumor to come back."

"That's perfect," Brenda said. "So, we want to have a baby with Daniel's sperm and the surrogate's egg?"

"No, you don't. That's asking for possible legal and custody problems. You're much better off making and freezing some embryos before you start hormone treatment."

"Is that safe for me?" Brenda asked.

"Good question. It does require a high level of estrogen to stimulate all those eggs, but it's much less of a risk than a nine-month pregnancy. You're willing to take the chance."

"So, we would be looking for an infertility doctor who does in vitro fertilization, as well as a surrogate?" Daniel asked.

"I wonder if the CEO of Beverly Hills Surrogacy Institute will refer us to anyone in particular," Brenda said.

"I can't imagine who," I commented, raising my eyebrow.

"What questions should we be asking?" Daniel said.

"You'll want to know how they recruit surrogates, who is currently available, if you can look at medical records before making a decision, and how much they charge."

"We should probably ask for details of the payment plan, and whether anything is covered by insurance," Daniel added. "Most couples, unless they are quite wealthy, would probably want to know."

"What if she asks who my doctors are?" Brenda said.

"I'll give you names of breast cancer specialists and gynecologists. You should have one of each memorized."

"That's perfect. Thanks, love." Daniel dug into his cheesecake.

Brenda helped herself to a chocolate cookie. When she finished her coffee, Brenda stood up. "I'd better head home. We have a busy day tomorrow."

"I'll pick you up at nine-thirty, at your apartment," Daniel said.

Brenda grinned. "I'll try and dress the part."

CHAPTER THIRTY-TWO

BRENDA LIVED IN AN APARTMENT building in Culver City. Daniel had never been there, despite their many years of working as a team. He rang the bell and his jaw dropped when she opened the door.

Brenda was wearing a long-sleeved, navy shirtwaist with a white collar and cuffs. A string of pearls adorned her neck, and her blonde hair, normally pulled back into a pony tail, had been blow-dried into a neat pageboy.

"I didn't know you owned a dress."

"It's my *going to church* outfit. My mother bought it for me last Christmas, in the fond hope that it would help me attract a husband in the congregation." She gave him a smug grin. "I've never seen you in a suit."

"I avoid them like the plague. Can you walk in those shoes?"

Brenda was wearing navy stilettos.

"I guess we'll find out." She grabbed a small, navy shoulder bag and locked the door behind her.

Daniel offered his arm, as she picked her way down the stairs.

"Well, dear," he said. "You certainly are dressing the part."

He opened the passenger door of his Mustang for her and she slid in. Daniel put the car in gear and headed north to Beverly Hills.

～

"And here we are," Daniel said, as he pulled the car into the parking lot.

The Beverly Hills Surrogacy Institute was in a modest office building on South Beverly Drive. The waiting room was elaborate. Daniel and Brenda opened the door to plush carpet, velvet-upholstered armchairs, a fruitwood coffee table and lots of mirrors. Professional photos of happy couples with their babies decorated the walls. An attractive receptionist, behind a glass window, greeted them, handed them some paperwork, and asked them to have a seat. Daniel filled out their false names, false address and phone number, read the privacy policy, and initialed the paper that made it clear they were financially responsible for all expenses associated with a surrogate pregnancy.

A few minutes later, they were escorted to an elegant office. Courtney Duchamps, attired in an off-white designer suit, shook their hands and invited them to sit on a loveseat with plump cushions. She sat opposite, in a wing chair.

"I'm so happy to meet you both," she gushed. "How can we help you?"

Brenda launched into her tale of breast cancer and how it had upended their plans to have a family. Daniel said that they were looking for a fertility doctor to help them store some embryos before his wife began her hormone therapy. They wanted to find a surrogate who could bear their baby.

"I can help you with both those things," Courtney replied. "One of the best fertility doctors in town is Kamran Nazari. Let me give you his card. Just say you were referred by me."

Daniel took the card and placed it carefully in his wallet.

"We have a large selection of willing surrogates for you to choose from. California law requires both the surrogate and the prospective parents to engage a surrogacy attorney, and to have a contract before proceeding with the pregnancy, so that your rights to child custody are firmly established. We have attorneys who work with us to make that process easy for you."

"How do we choose a surrogate?" Brenda asked.

Courtney swiveled toward her desk and reached for a large, black binder.

"Here are photographs and biographies of our currently available surrogates. You can look at them at your leisure, in our conference room. Once you have selected one or two who interest you, we can arrange for you to meet and interview them, and for your obstetrician to review the medical records of your first choice, before a contract is signed."

"What about the financial arrangements?" Daniel asked. "How much will this cost us?"

"That depends on who you choose as your surrogate. A first-time surrogate is less expensive than one who has previously delivered. The total includes our agency fee, compensation for the surrogate and her expenses during the pregnancy, fertility clinic fee, and legal fees."

She reached for a manila envelope and handed it to Daniel. "Here is a detailed breakdown. We can arrange for monthly payments during the pregnancy, and for a loan if you don't happen to have the cash available."

"Thank you," Daniel said. "Hopefully a loan won't be necessary."

"Our parents are anxious for a grandchild. They're helping us," Brenda said.

"That's so nice of them," said Courtney. "Why don't I take you to the conference room, so you can spend some time reviewing everything, and then I'll be available for questions once you've finished."

The conference room was small, with a table that seated four, and well stocked with coffee, tea and coffee cake. Brenda poured out cups for both of them, and Daniel helped himself to a cinnamon roll.

Brenda began flipping through the binder.

"Slow down," Daniel said. "I want to photograph each page and send it to Izzy for a real background check."

"They only provide first names," Brenda said.

"That's what facial recognition software is for. Never underestimate Izzy."

While Daniel was photographing, Brenda turned her attention to the financial information. She gave a low whistle.

"What?" Daniel said.

"Listen to this. Forty grand for a first-time surrogate, a clothing allowance, an embryo transfer fee, a monthly allowance for the surrogate and a housekeeping budget. Then, they charge for psychological screening for the parents and the surrogate, and criminal background checks for everyone."

"Well, we can do that part," Daniel said.

"You missed the point. If they do it, they can leave out information. And there's more. Legal fees, about 15 grand, a fee for a psychological support group for the surrogate, her health insurance, and all the fees for the IVF, which aren't specified. We would definitely have to ask our parents for help."

"This is clearly not for poor people," Daniel said, closing the binder and hitting send on his phone. "Let's thank Courtney and get out of here."

They exited the consult room and walked to Courtney's office. The door was open. She looked up and beckoned them in.

"Thank you so much, Miss Duchamps," Daniel said. "We've made notes on several surrogates who interest us. We need to talk to our families about the finances and then we'll be back in touch to schedule some interviews."

"No questions?" she asked.

"I think we're good," Brenda said. "We hope to see you again very soon."

As they exited the office, Daniel turned to Brenda. "You did a great job as my surrogate wife."

"I'm not so sure," Brenda said, hobbling to the elevator. "Hannah would never wear stilettos."

CHAPTER THIRTY-THREE

I GOT TO MY OFFICE MIDMORNING, after completing two brief operations at the hospital's outpatient Surgery Center. Ruth was at her desk, working her way through a large pile of paper. I motioned for her to come into my consult room and closed the door.

"What?" she asked.

"I need you to draw my blood for a pregnancy test."

"Isn't it a little early?" Ruth asked. "It's only been a week since your egg retrieval."

"You know patience isn't my strong suit. If no pregnancy hormone shows up, we can repeat it next week."

"Only if you promise me not to freak out if it's negative," Ruth said.

"I promise. We should probably call for a stat pickup, so we get the results this afternoon."

Ruth rolled her eyes at me and opened the door. "Stay put and I'll be back with a syringe," she said.

I sat there with my fingers crossed. A positive pregnancy test would be the best news I could possibly bring to Daniel.

CHAPTER THIRTY-FOUR

DANIEL AND BRENDA ENTERED THE office to a loud wolf whistle. As soon as Brenda sat at her desk, she traded in the high heels for a pair of trainers. Daniel brought them both mugs of coffee and some doughnuts.

"Hey guys, I've got some info," Izzy yelled from his desk. The two of them walked over.

"I tracked down the incorporation information for the Surrogacy Institute. There are three partners, Duchamps, Ian Price and Kamran Nazari."

"Interesting," Brenda said. "Is there anything illegal about Price and Nazari referring patients to a surrogacy agency they own? Or vice versa?"

"I don't think it's any different from surgeons being partners in surgery centers. Although, they may be legally required to disclose that information," Izzy said.

"Then why would Louise have objected?" Daniel asked.

"Maybe she didn't like Courtney," Brenda said. "I wonder if Louise knew anything about Courtney's past? Or maybe it just felt a little sleazy. From what you told me, Louise was a class act."

"That she was," Daniel commented.

"Or maybe, Louise found out that some of the surrogates were former escorts," Izzy said, with a satisfied expression.

"Ha! I knew it!" Brenda said. "You find proof?"

"I've only had time to do facial recognition on one surrogate, but yes. I've sent your photos over to Vice to see if any of those guys recognize the faces. It seems Courtney figured out it was more lucrative, and legal, to run a surrogacy agency with her former escorts, than risk being shut down and jailed for being a Madam."

"That would certainly explain Louise's objections," Brenda said. "Maybe she threatened to shut down this deal and her partners killed her. Judging from the financial arrangements, they stood to get pretty rich from this agency."

"Let's wait for some more ammunition from Vice, and then you and I will go and re-interview the partners," Daniel said.

"Great. But before I do anything else, I'm going to go to my locker and change," Brenda said.

When Daniel got home, Hannah greeted him at the door with a long kiss. There was a glass of wine, brie and crackers, and some truffle pâté, waiting in the den.

"It's not my birthday," Daniel said.

"True, but I thought my positive pregnancy test was worth celebrating."

Daniel threw his arms around her. "For real? We're pregnant? That's wonderful!"

"Don't get too excited. We have to see a heartbeat at six

weeks, and I need to get through the first trimester before I'm sure it's a go. We can't tell anyone yet."

"Not even your mother?"

"Are you kidding? If my mother finds out I'm pregnant before we get married, she'll go ballistic."

"Well, then." Daniel said. "Hadn't we better finally set a date? How much lead time do we need to plan a wedding?"

"It depends on how big a wedding. I'd like to get married on our beautiful back deck, with just our immediate family and closest friends. I think six to eight weeks should do it."

"Any ideas on who should marry us, parental religious preferences notwithstanding?"

"How about a Universal Life Minister? I love the fact that your best friend can get ordained online, and you can be married by someone who knows you, instead of a Rent-A-Rabbi," Hannah said. "Why don't I ask Andrea, and make sure she can do it, before we pick a day? Then I'll send out a "Save the Date" email. I figure the end of October should be just right."

"Sounds perfect, sweetheart," Daniel said.

CHAPTER THIRTY-FIVE

I WAS ENORMOUSLY RELIEVED WHEN the weekend arrived. I knew that Daniel was frustrated and anxious because, after a week, he was no closer to solving Louise's murder, but I persuaded him that two days of relaxation might clear his brain and generate some new directions to follow.

The first thing I did, Saturday morning, was to call my best friend Andrea.

"Andrea, will you marry me?"

"Darling, dearly as I love you, I'm already married."

"Let me rephrase that. Will you get ordained online and marry us? Daniel and I want to set a date."

"Why didn't you say so?" Andrea said. "I'd be honored, and I promise not to tell any embarrassing stories about you."

She and I and Daniel coordinated our calendars and selected the last Saturday in October. Then, we made a date for the following weekend to go wedding dress shopping. I always shop more efficiently (and spend more money) with Andrea egging me on. We decided to invite Ruth as well. As a threesome, we were formidable.

The next thing I did, was to make blueberry pancakes for Daniel and Zoe, and break the news.

"Zoe, we have something to tell you. Next month, Daniel and I are going to be married. Would you like to be my flower girl?"

A huge smile lit up her face. "Can I be maid of honor?"

I'd had Ruth in mind for that role, but Zoe outranked her.

"You absolutely can."

Zoe turned to Daniel. "When you and Mommy are married, is it okay if I call you Daddy?"

Daniel melted. He leaned over, cupped her chin in his hand, and deposited a kiss on her forehead. "You can call me Daddy right now," he said.

After breakfast, Daniel and I started work on the guest list. The first priority was his parents and mine, and his sister and her husband. Andrea and her husband, Jonathan, were on my list, as well as Ruth and her husband, Arthur, a food and wine aficionado who owned several very successful restaurants. I wanted to talk to him about catering the wedding dinner, as well. Daniel added Brenda and her partner, Marcy; and Izzy Washington and his wife; a perfect number for an intimate event.

We spent the rest of the weekend not discussing Louise. We took Zoe to the latest animated movie. We sat out on the back deck, in the sun, and read novels. We made "To Do"

lists for our wedding, and called everyone on our guest list and told them to save the date. After Zoe was in bed, we made love two nights in a row, and by Monday morning, both of us were reenergized.

CHAPTER THIRTY-SIX

Brenda was already at her desk when Daniel arrived at the office.

"I was glad to hear that you and Hannah finally set a date. It's about time."

Daniel slid into his seat and booted up his computer. "I really needed this weekend. I was wiped out."

"I know what you mean," Brenda said. "I've got a few ideas. I just looked up each of the partner's car registrations. Ian Price drives a black Audi A8, and Nazari's got a red Porsche Carrera."

"Of course, he does," said Daniel.

"I've got the license plates. I thought we could check the traffic cameras on Pico and see if either of them were in the vicinity of Louise's car at the time of the murder."

"That's a lot of footage."

"I've got Louise's Honda at seven-twenty p.m., passing the traffic light near the street where she parked. I'm scanning very slowly, looking for the Porsche now. I emailed you the video. You could look for the Audi."

"Will do. Any news from Vice?" Daniel asked, as he opened his email.

"Yeah. They were able to identify about half your photos. The other half are probably women who were recruited from the website."

"Great, that gives us enough ammunition for a chat with the partners. I'll give the office a call and tell them to expect us at lunchtime," Daniel said.

This was going to be a little awkward. Hannah was pregnant, thanks to Westside Fertility. And even though she had only seen Louise and Nori Tanaka, she would still be going to that office several more times, before Ruth took over the care of her pregnancy. And here he was, suspecting two of Louise's partners of murder. Perhaps he should let Brenda take the lead on those interviews.

CHAPTER THIRTY-SEVEN

I GOT TO THE OFFICE IN A VERY MELLOW mood, and emailed Nori Tanaka to tell her the good news. She asked me to repeat the blood test in a week, and to come into her office for an ultrasound in two weeks. That was too soon for a heartbeat, but we should be able to see a small sac and the very beginning of fetal development if everything was proceeding on course.

My receptionist handed me a printout of my morning schedule and told me she'd squeezed in an emergency visit from Victoria Bachman.

"She said she was having cramps and was afraid she was going to miscarry."

This news did not make my day. All the other patients on my schedule were women I really enjoyed seeing, and dealing with Victoria would ruin my good mood. It isn't often I develop a strong antipathy for a patient, but her narcissism had rubbed me the wrong way. I took a deep breath and tried to feel more empathic.

My nurse notified me that Victoria was waiting for me in an examination room.

"Good morning," I said, as I walked in. "I hear you're having some cramping."

"I'm going to lose these goddamn babies and it will be ten grand wasted. Not to mention the fact that my ex will be delighted."

"Let's not jump to conclusions," I said. "Let me examine you first. Are you bleeding?"

"No."

"Are you having any pain when you urinate?"

"No, but I'm peeing every five minutes."

"Did you leave us a urine sample?"

"Yes, I filled a whole jar," she said.

I coaxed her into the stirrups and gently inserted a speculum. There was no bleeding. I did a bacterial culture and reached for my ultrasound. The twins were frolicking happily with strong heartbeats."

"So far, so good," I said. "I'm going to go to the lab and take a look at your urine."

One peek in the microscope told me she had a urinary tract infection.

"No worries," I announced. "It's just a UTI. I'll give you some antibiotics and you'll be fine in twenty-four hours."

"That's a relief. Phillip is behaving like such an asshole. He keeps telling me he won't pay a penny in child support and talking about what a bitch Louise Waldman was. He took an instant dislike to her the first time we went to her office. He wanted me to switch doctors."

"That's odd," I said. "Louise was such a nice person. Any idea why?"

"Not a clue. Luckily I didn't listen to him. Sometimes, I wonder why I married him in the first place. The only things that interest him are working out in his damned gym, and outdoor sports. I'd rather shoot myself than put on a pack and sleep in a tent, or mountain climb. You'd think that, at his age, he would stop doing the stuff he did at twenty and behave like a grownup."

"What do you like to do?" I asked.

"I like to go to movies, go shopping, spend the evening in clubs and party with my friends. Phillip is the least social man I know."

"It doesn't sound as if you were a match made in heaven," I commented. "What was the attraction?"

She shrugged her shoulders. "He was hot-looking when we met, rich, drove a sports car, and bought me lots of great jewelry. He was also married. I should never have encouraged him to leave his first wife."

"Does he have other children?"

"Not a one. Wife number one was infertile. He wanted a son to leave his gym empire to. Now, he's apparently changed his mind."

"Perhaps he'll feel differently if one of the twins is a boy."

"I made sure both were female. I told Dr. Waldman to implant only girl embryos. I didn't want to give the bastard the satisfaction," Victoria said.

"Did he try to talk you into having an abortion?" I asked

"Hell, no. Phillip thinks women who have abortions are going straight to hell. He would have preferred for God to arrange a miscarriage."

Victoria slid off the exam table and into her Louboutin pumps. "If he thinks he's going to get away without paying for these babies, he has another thing coming."

"I'll check your culture results and call you if there's any problem," I said. "In the meantime, take it easy and make an appointment for a month from now."

She flashed me a red-lipsticked smile.

CHAPTER THIRTY-EIGHT

DANIEL AND BRENDA PULLED INTO THE parking lot for Westside Fertility.

"I'd like you to handle these interviews," Daniel said. "I'm trying to keep a low profile."

"Any special reason?" Brenda asked.

"These people are Hannah's colleagues. She always sent her fertility patients to Louise, and the fact that two of Louise's partners have motives for murder makes it a little uncomfortable for me."

"Understood. I wish we had found their cars on the videos. We have motive but not the slightest bit of evidence that either one of them was anywhere near the murder scene."

"Don't remind me," Daniel said.

The two of them got in the elevator, which deposited them in a large, well-appointed waiting room.

Brenda approached the receptionist. "We're Detectives Jordan and Ross. We're here to talk to Dr. Nazari and Dr. Price. We can start with whoever is free first."

"I remember you," the receptionist smiled. "Any progress solving Dr. Waldman's murder?"

"We're working on it," Brenda said. "No news yet."

The receptionist picked up the phone and announced that Dr. Price was free. "His consult room is the second on the left," she said, buzzing them into the interior space.

They knocked on Dr. Price's door and were told to come in.

Ian Price was wearing scrubs and eating a tuna sandwich when they entered. He patted his lips with a napkin, took a swig of Coca Cola from a can, and motioned them to sit down.

"How can I assist the LAPD today," he said, smiling.

Daniel took out a pen and notebook, and Brenda leaned forward in her chair. "We understand that you and Dr. Nazari have recently formed a partnership with Beverly Hills Surrogacy Institute," she said.

"That is true, but what does it have to do with Louise's death?"

"Was Dr. Waldman invited to join this partnership?" Brenda asked.

"She wasn't interested," Price took a large bite of his sandwich and chewed vigorously.

"Was that because she disapproved of it?"

Price finished chewing. Brenda waited.

"Louise was, financially, very risk averse and wasn't interested in branching out in any way," he said.

"Was it possible that Louise disapproved because she found out that your other partner, Miss Duchamps, had previously run an escort service and was now offering some of her girls as surrogates?"

Price had just taken another mouthful of Coke and began to sputter. "That's absurd."

"That's what the police records show, Dr. Price. Did you and Louise Waldman argue about your business plans?"

"Of course not. My plans were none of her business. There is nothing illegal about my participating in a surrogacy agency. If she didn't like it, she didn't have to send her patients there."

"Was she trying to stop the two of you from proceeding with what was clearly a very lucrative business arrangement? She was the senior partner. Did she threaten to dissolve your partnership if you proceeded?"

Ian Price leaned forward over his desk. "I see where you're going with this," he said, "and you don't have a shred of evidence."

"Where are we going?" Brenda asked.

"You're implying that I had a motive for getting Louise out of the way, but you couldn't be more wrong."

"Remind us again, Dr. Price," Daniel said. "Where were you on the night Louise was murdered?"

"I already told you. I arrived home from our Valley office at six-thirty, and stayed there until the next morning."

"Can anyone verify that?" Brenda asked. "Was someone there with you?"

Ian hesitated, clasping and unclasping his hands on his desk. "My housekeeper, Imelda, was at home when I arrived and left shortly afterwards. I made a number of phone calls from my landline to patients. No doubt you can confirm those."

"No young lady spending the night?"

"I'm divorced," Price said. "There are frequently young ladies spending the night, but not that night."

"What time did you leave your house?"

"I usually leave about seven in the morning. I have one of those video doorbells with a motion detector. It records everyone who comes to the front door. You can see me entering and leaving." Price reached for his cell phone, brought up the Ring app, and passed it to Brenda.

On the date in question, a video showed Price entering at 6:34 p.m. At 6:45 p.m., a woman left the house. The next video was at 7:05 a.m. and showed Price locking his door and walking to his car.

"Do you have a garage?" Daniel asked.

"Yes, what about it?"

"I'm wondering why you go in and out of your house by the front door, instead of driving into the garage and entering that way."

"You obviously haven't seen my garage. I'd have trouble fitting a bicycle into it, let alone a large Audi. Anyway, I have a paved front courtyard to park in."

Brenda reached into her purse and pulled out a plastic evidence envelope. She slipped Price's phone into it. "I'm afraid we're going to have to take this as evidence, until we've downloaded your video."

"Shit, how do you expect me to function without my cell phone?"

"I'm sure you'll figure it out," Daniel said. "We'll get back to you."

The two of them left Price's office and walked down the hall to Nazari's consult room. When they knocked and opened the door, he was on the phone. He pointed in the direction of two chairs and completed his call.

"I hope this won't take long. I have to leave in fifteen minutes. I'm meeting someone for lunch."

"We'll try to be brief," Brenda said. "We're interested in your business relationship with Beverly Hills Surrogacy Institute. Did you argue about it with Louise Waldman?"

"I argued with Louise every time Ian and I wanted to expand the reach of the practice. She had no financial vision."

"Is it possible that she objected to you partnering with a woman who had a police record and who was using escorts as surrogates?"

"I don't know what you are talking about," Nazari said.

"I think you do, Dr. Nazari, and if Louise had exposed that fact, your career would have been significantly damaged. Were you very angry at her?"

"What are you implying?"

Daniel stopped taking notes and leaned forward. "We're implying that her death was very convenient, for you and for your associate, Dr. Price."

"I'm not discussing this any further," Nazari said. "You can talk to my lawyer. I want both of you out of my office, now."

"You'll be hearing from us," Brenda said, as they both stood and headed for the door.

Neither of them said anything until they reached the car.

"This is so frustrating," Daniel said. "It's certainly not out of the question that Ian Price could have left his house by another entrance, but how could he have known where Louise was? The same holds for Nazari. There's something we're missing."

"The killer could have been hired by FPA and told where

to find her." Brenda said. "Or he may have been stalking her for some other reason."

"Whoever it was, he must have had a place nearby to torture her. Let's go back to the station and look at the camera footage again."

"What are we looking for?"

"I want to track down the license plates of every car that drove past the nearest traffic camera on Pico, within five minutes of Louise."

CHAPTER THIRTY-NINE

"DADDY'S HOME!" ZOE RAN DOWN THE hall to the front door, the moment she heard Daniel's footsteps.

He entered the kitchen carrying her on his hip, with a large grin on his face. I decided not to raise any subject that would upset his mood.

Emilia, our beloved housekeeper and nanny, had left us a salad and homemade pasta sauce, leaving me with the culinary challenge of boiling some linguine. I was up to the job, and the three of us had a relaxing dinner, after which, Daniel took care of the dishes and I helped with Zoe's math homework.

Once she was in bed, and we were ensconced in our most comfortable den chairs, I decided to pass on my information.

"I learned something interesting today from Victoria Bachman. In the course of her office visit she mentioned that her almost ex-husband was very anti-abortion, and that he had taken an instant dislike to Louise, on their first visit. He tried to persuade Victoria to switch doctors. I'm wondering if he could have been associated with the FPA."

"Now that is interesting. I'll run it by the FBI. They've got Karl Schmidt's phones and computer. Maybe we'll get lucky, and they'll find a link to Phillip Bachman."

"Something else," I said. "Victoria was complaining that the only things Phillip liked to do were outdoor sports, like mountaineering. He reminded me of Louise. She loved outdoor sports. Is it possible they could have run into one another earlier,?"

"You're suggesting that the instant dislike was really an old dislike?"

"Possibly," I said. "We should look for some links."

Daniel smiled, walked over to my chair, and leaned down to kiss me. "We should indeed."

He drew me up and out of my chair, and kissed me again. "How about we get started on that tomorrow?"

____

CHAPTER FORTY

WHEN DANIEL GOT TO THE STATION THE next morning, the first thing he did was call Brian Anderson.

"Glad you called," Brian said. "I was just emailing you some information."

"What did you find?"

"We went over Karl Schmidt's phones, both the throw-away and his smart phone, as well as his computer. We also checked the disposable phones from his daughter and the skin heads."

"And?"

"All of Schmidt's outgoing calls, for the month prior to their meeting, were to his bomb suppliers. None of the skin-heads made any outgoing calls on their disposable phones, nor did Karen-Kay. There were several calls to another number, after the meeting, but none of those calls connected. I'm assuming they were to Louise's disposable phone. If Schmidt hired or persuaded someone to get rid of Louise, he didn't do it by telephone."

Damn it. Another dead end. Daniel restrained himself

from hitting his desktop with a fist. "What about his smart phone and computer?"

"We're tracking down every person he called. For the most part, they seem to be parishioners. I'm sending you all the names, in case anything rings a bell in your murder investigation. I'm also emailing you a bunch of videos."

"Videos of what?"

"Protests," Brian said. "The FPA spends most of its efforts organizing demonstrations at abortion clinics. Most of them are in Orange County, but a few have been in Los Angeles. They frequently target Planned Parenthood, or any other clinic that does a large volume of terminations. We've had agents taking videos for some time, and we've identified all the regulars. I'm planning to bring them all in and question them. They're on the list I sent you."

"Are the regulars his parishioners?" Daniel asked.

"Some are, not all. We think there's a two- tier structure. The bulk of the FPA members function as protestors, or lobby legislators to pass anti-abortion bills. Then there's the small inner circle that plans more radical action."

Daniel booted up his computer and opened his email. Anderson's files were waiting. "Have they ever set off a bomb or attacked a doctor before?"

"Not that we know of. This may have been their first attempt."

"Thanks, Brian. We'll have a look at these and see if anything helpful emerges. One more thing. Could you see if the FBI has a file on a Phillip Bachman? He's the guy who sued Louise for malpractice. We just found out that he was virulently anti-abortion and wondered if there was an FPA connection."

"Will do. I'll get back to you."

Daniel motioned to Brenda and Izzy to join him at his desk.

"What's up?" Izzy said.

Daniel brought them up to date. "Could you do a deep background check on Bachman?" he asked Izzy. "Brenda and I will go through these videos, and the list of regulars, to see if anything looks promising."

"Sure boss," Izzy said. "

The list of regular protestors consisted of some thirty names, most with Orange County addresses. None of them were familiar. Daniel moved on to the videos. The Los Angeles file was smaller, so he started there. Each protest had about a dozen people carrying homemade signs that said things like "Baby Killer" and "If You Abort Your Baby, You'll Go To Hell." Some of them wore FPA T-shirts. The first demonstration was at a small clinic in Culver City, the second at a Planned Parenthood in Van Nuys. Daniel paused frequently, examining faces, looking for anything familiar.

"Daniel, look at this," Brenda said.

He got up and peered over her shoulder. "She was staring at a large demonstration in front of Planned Parenthood's downtown headquarters. Police and security guards were escorting patients past a larger than usual group of protestors. Brenda replayed the footage. Standing at the edge of the protest group, not carrying a sign, was a balding, gray-haired man. He turned his head toward the clinic entrance, affording them a good view of his profile. Brenda hit pause.

"Isn't that Phillip Bachman?" she asked.

CHAPTER FORTY-ONE

Aﬀﬀﬀ﬩FTER DROPPING ZOE OFF AT THE Waverly School on Mulholland Drive, I fought the Tuesday morning traffic to the hospital. I quickly made post-surgical rounds and walked across the street to my office.

"Phone call for you," my receptionist said, as I came through the door. "It's a Phillip Bachman calling."

"This is Dr. Kline. How can I help you?"

"I understand you're taking care of my wife, Victoria. I'm calling to find out how the pregnancy is progressing."

"I'm sorry, Mr. Bachman, but Federal HIPAA regulations prohibit me from discussing any patient's medical status, even with a family member, unless I have written permission."

"You know this is an illegal pregnancy? I'm suing Dr. Waldman for implanting our embryos after we filed for divorce. I'll be suing you too, for wrongful birth, if you deliver her."

Could this day get any more annoying? I'd never been sued for just doing my obstetrical job.

"If you're threatening to sue me, I can't continue this conversation. Goodbye, Mr. Bachman."

I hung up. I was going to have to report this encounter to my malpractice carrier.

Ruth poked her head into my doorway.

"What's up?" I asked.

"What's up with you? You're looking upset."

"A patient's husband just threatened to sue me if I deliver his wife. I guess he's hoping to intimidate every obstetrician in town, so she has to deliver her twins squatting in a field somewhere. He obviously wants those babies dead."

"Wow, that's a new twist," Ruth said. "I was just popping in to let you know that Arthur was thrilled you want him to cater your wedding. He's going to email you a few sample menus."

My upcoming wedding had almost slipped my mind. Nice to know my friends were taking care of the details.

"That's the only nice thing that's happened so far today. Tell your husband I'm sending a hug and a big thank you," I said.

My next patient was a new one, a juvenile diabetic who wanted my advice on fertility. An exam and a rapid laboratory test revealed that her blood sugars were sky high, and she was already at least six weeks pregnant. I cursed the idiot who had removed her IUD before getting her diabetes under control, and arranged for an immediate admission to the hospital, along with several consults. This occupied a large chunk of time and I was running half an hour late when my receptionist signaled me.

"Message for you, Dr. Kline," she said, as I walked past her desk.

I took the slip of paper from her hand. The message was from Frances Conners. I called back.

"I've got your yearbook," she announced, "and you owe me more than cheesecake. You have no idea how many boxes I had to go through to locate it."

I laughed. "How about Daniel and I treat you to an expensive dinner? Have you had a chance to look through it?"

"Our class at Berkeley was huge. It's going to take hours. I'll try to make a start tonight."

"Great. Dinner Saturday? You can pick your favorite foodie place. Our treat. We really appreciate the effort."

I looked at my schedule and pulled up the next medical record onto my screen. I was going to have to wait until my lunch break to call Daniel.

CHAPTER FORTY-TWO

D ANIEL WAS PERUSING PHILLIP Bachman's Facebook page. It was amazing how much personal information people posted online. Facebook gave Daniel the creeps. He always thought of it as a stalker's menu.

Phillip had posted many photos of himself, engaging in manly activities, flexing his biceps, doing chin-ups and push-ups. A few were bare-chested, showing off his sixty-year-old six-pack. There were also party pictures with Phillip in the company of much younger, exceedingly fit, pretty women. He listed his status as separated, with a post that his divorce was in process.

His profile was available as well, on several online dating sites; eHarmony, Plenty of Fish and, of course, Tinder. He described himself as a very successful businessman looking for a relationship with a thin, athletic woman who enjoyed outdoor as well as indoor sports.

"Yuck," commented Brenda.

"Maybe. But I bet he gets lots of responses," Daniel said.

"No accounting for taste."

"Hey, Daniel," Izzy called from across the room. "Come here, you guys. I've got something interesting."

"On Bachman?"

"Yeah. I've been checking his financials and his property. Guy owns a dozen low-end gyms which generate a fair amount of cash. He's definitely well off. Got married two years ago and bought a nice house in south Beverly Hills. Looks like the wife is living in the house, because he rented a place two months ago, south of Pico, and just a few blocks from the body dump."

"No shit," Brenda said, looking over Izzy's shoulder.

He had Zillow on his screen. It showed a modest Spanish-style, one-story bungalow, two bedrooms, two baths, not currently listed for sale. The estimated value was $975,000.

"I can't believe anyone would pay that much money for such a tiny house," Izzy said. "Even the rental price is crazy."

"Welcome to Los Angeles real estate," Daniel said.

"Think a judge would give us a warrant to search his house?" Brenda asked.

"Not without more evidence," Daniel said. "But Bachman has definitely moved way up on my suspect list."

"Why would he want to kill Louise? If she's dead, he's unlikely to win a malpractice settlement."

"There's got to be something else," Daniel said. "How about you and I scope out the neighborhood, and have a chat with the neighbors?"

CHAPTER FORTY-THREE

DANIEL AND BRENDA TOOK AN unmarked car from the police lot, and drove to the street where Louise's car had been found. It was a quiet residential neighborhood, once full of one-story, mostly Spanish-style homes, now undergoing mansionization. A number of large two-story homes occupied almost full lots, often out of scale with their neighbors.

"I can see what's happening to prices in this area of town," Brenda commented.

"Everywhere," Daniel said.

As they drove further south, toward the freeway, the homes became smaller and somewhat shabbier. Phillip Bachman's house was three blocks south of Pico and a block west.

"We're only three blocks from where Louise's body was dumped," Brenda said.

Daniel drove slowly down Bachman's street.

"You wouldn't happen to know what kind of a car he drives?" Daniel asked.

"Of course, I do. It's a silver, Mercedes E Class Coupe."

"The house is coming up on the right. See if the car is in the driveway or on the street."

The house was a small Spanish bungalow with faded turquoise trim, in need of a paint job. The front yard was mostly gravel, with a few cactus plants and some succulents.

"Looks like he hasn't done much to make the place home, since he moved in. I don't see a car, although it could be in the garage."

"Let's ring the bell, and if he isn't home, we can circle the house and see if any of the windows are uncovered," Daniel said.

"What are you planning to do if he answers the door?"

"Find out if he has an alibi for the night of Louise's death. Then we can canvass the neighbors."

Daniel parked two houses down and they walked up to the front door. He rang the doorbell several times, but there was no answer.

"He's probably at the gym," Brenda said.

"Let's take a look around."

They walked up the driveway, peering into windows. They were covered with shades, but most of them weren't pulled all the way down. Daniel peered into a 1950's kitchen with dishes piled in the sink, a living room with a fireplace, a large flat-screen TV and what looked like newly purchased cheap leather furniture. They came around to a concrete back yard, with an unattached garage. Brenda looked through a dirty window on the side.

"Lots of junk. No car," she said.

They continued to circle the house. The back bedroom had curtains on the window, and those were pulled tight. A second bedroom appeared to be functioning as an office. Daniel saw a desk, a half-empty bookcase, and unpacked cardboard boxes.

"Looks like a fixer-upper that hasn't been fixed up yet," Daniel said.

"Let's go visit the neighbors," said Brenda.

Interviewing the neighbors was an exercise in futility. None of them knew Phillip Bachman, or could remember seeing a woman who looked like Louise the night of the murder. Daniel hadn't expected anything else. People didn't normally stare out their front windows, watching the street late at night, and neither of the next door neighbors had so much as exchanged a word with the new arrival. Although there were more than a few comments about how it would be nice if the landlord painted the house and cleaned up the landscaping on the front yard. Most residents on the street appeared to take good care of their property.

It was late afternoon by the time they finished, and the two of them decided to return to the station and head home.

CHAPTER FORTY-FOUR

T HE NEXT MORNING, I MADE EARLY rounds on my pregnant diabetic, whose blood sugars were now in the normal range. I wrote orders to discharge her, and told her to make an appointment to see me the following week. I then returned to my office, hoping for an uneventful day. It was not to be.

At 11:30 a.m., my phone intercom buzzed.

"Dr. Kline, there's a call from the Beverly Hills Police Department. Should I put it through?"

"Yes, please." I picked up the phone. "This is Dr. Kline. Can I help you?"

"This is Sergeant Marilyn Sanders. I'm calling about your patient, Victoria Bachman."

"What about her?"

"She was found dead this morning by her housekeeper. I found two prescription bottles on her bedside table under your name, a prenatal vitamin and an antibiotic, so I'm calling to see if you have information that might be pertinent."

"Oh, my God! I just saw her yesterday. How did she die?"

My patients were mostly young and healthy. They weren't supposed to die. Could this be yet another murder?

"It looks like a natural death. She was found in bed, looking as if she were asleep. There weren't any obvious signs of violence and the housekeeper said the front door was locked. Did she have any serious medical problems, or did you get any hint that she might be depressed or suicidal?"

"Let me look at her chart." I accessed my electronic medical records and typed in her name. I didn't recall any significant medical history, and my review confirmed my memory. "She has no history of any medical issues. Will there be an autopsy?"

"Yes, of course. We always do an autopsy when someone dies at home for no obvious reason. Often it's an overdose, but we didn't find any traces of narcotics or alcohol in the home. What about suicide, doctor? What's your assessment?"

"In all honesty, I didn't know her very well. I'd only seen her twice, but I didn't get the slightest hint of depression. She was in the midst of a nasty divorce, and I can't imagine that she'd kill herself and give her soon-to-be ex-husband the satisfaction."

"Do you know anything about him?"

I knew a good deal about Phillip Bachman, and I struggled for a few moments, trying to decide if sharing my information was breeching doctor-patient confidentiality or Daniel's. I finally decided to share everything I'd learned on my own.

"The Bachmans were infertility patients of Dr. Louise Waldman. They produced a number of embryos for in vitro fertilization before they decided to get divorced. The embryos were supposed to have been destroyed, but

Victoria was implanted with two of them before Dr. Waldman was notified of the split. He sued her for malpractice, and just yesterday, called my office and threatened to sue me for wrongful birth, if I delivered his wife's twins."

"An angry husband is always number one on the suspect list when a woman is murdered. But, at the moment, this doesn't look suspicious," the Sergeant said.

"There's something else you should know. Dr. Louise Waldman was murdered a week ago, and Phillip Bachman is one of many persons of interest in the investigation. Homicide Detective Daniel Ross of the LAPD is in charge. I have his cell phone number. You might find it valuable to touch base."

I hoped that was tactful enough.

"You seem to know quite a bit about that investigation," she said, a trace of suspicion in her voice.

"Dr. Waldman was a friend and colleague, and I'm engaged to Detective Ross, so I know whatever he's permitted to tell me."

"I see. Do you think Detective Ross would want to come and check out the scene before we remove the body?"

"I think he'd appreciate being asked, and would be grateful for anything you might be able to contribute to his case."

"No problem. Why don't you give me the number and I'll give him a call."

CHAPTER FORTY-FIVE

D ANIEL'S CELL PHONE RANG AS HE AND Brenda were deciding on their next move for the day. The number was unfamiliar.

Daniel took the call.

"Are you going to tell me what's going on?" Brenda said, as he concluded the conversation.

"We're going to Beverly Hills. Victoria Bachman's been found dead in her bedroom. The BHPD called Hannah because they found medication under her name, and she suggested they call me."

"Murder?"

"Unclear. The cop who called didn't think so, but invited us to view the body before they take it to the coroner."

"Does Phillip know?"

"I hope not. I'd like to see his reaction when he hears the news."

The Bachman home was a substantial English Tudor, two blocks south of Wilshire, in Beverly Hills. There was a lush lawn, tall hedges and several magnolia trees. A patrolman stood in front of the elaborate wooden door, which was slightly ajar. Daniel and Brenda identified themselves and were shown inside, where they were greeted by a tall, young woman in uniform.

"I'm Sergeant Sanders," she said, holding out her hand.

Daniel shook it, and introduced Brenda.

"Come on upstairs."

Daniel and Brenda both put on shoe covers, from a box at the entryway, and latex gloves, then followed Sanders up a curved wooden stairway to the master suite. The room was large and elaborately decorated. There was plush white carpet on the floor and royal blue silk drapes, tied back with gold cord, on the windows. The center of the room was occupied by a canopied, king-sized bed.

Victoria Bachman's body lay on her back, blonde hair spread out on a pillow. She was covered with a white silk duvet, her arms draped over the covers. The lacy black straps of her nightgown were visible.

"She almost looks posed," Brenda commented.

"I was thinking the same thing," Daniel said, as he approached the bed.

He examined both arms, noting that the surface touching the bed was purple with pooled blood, which could also be glimpsed on her upper back. He touched one arm carefully and then attempted to flex it.

"Rigor mortis has certainly set in," he said. "It looks as if she died in bed." He glanced at his watch. It was 12:40 p.m. "When was she last seen alive?"

"The housekeeper phoned and spoke to her at about

nine p.m., to confirm that Mrs. Bachman expected her to come the next day.

Daniel bent over Victoria's body and looked carefully at her face and neck. Then he opened her eyelids and examined the whites of her eyes. Tiny hemorrhages from broken capillaries were visible.

"Sergeant, have you called in a crime team?"

"I haven't. Do I need to?"

"I think she's been suffocated, probably with a pillow. You can tell by the appearance of her eyes."

Sergeant Sanders looked, then reached for her cell. "I'll get on it right now. Thanks."

When Sanders completed her call, the three of them left the bedroom, closing the door behind them.

"Is the woman who found the body still here?" Daniel asked.

"She's in the kitchen with one of our officers. We asked her to stay until you got here, in case you had additional questions."

"Thank you," Daniel said. "Why don't we question her together? Has anyone notified the ex-husband?"

"Not yet," Sanders said.

The Bachman's housekeeper, Natalie Contreras, was seated at the kitchen table, nursing a cup of tea. She was a stout, sturdy-looking woman in her fifties, with short, dark hair streaked with gray. Her eyes were red and puffy, and she was gripping the mug tightly, as if to steady her hands. A female Beverly Hills police officer was seated opposite her.

Daniel approached. "Mrs. Contreras, I'm Detective Ross

from the LAPD. Thank you for waiting to talk to me. I just have a few questions."

Mrs. Contreras looked up at him and lowered the cup to the table. She reached into her purse for a tissue and wiped her eyes.

"What you want to know?" Her voice was soft, with just a hint of a Spanish accent.

"How long have you worked for the Bachmans?"

"Five years."

"Are you here every day?"

"I come twice a week, usually eleven o'clock in the morning. Mrs. Bachman liked to sleep late."

"And Mr. Bachman?"

"He was never here when I come. Sometimes, he come home early in the afternoon."

"When was the last time you saw Mr. Bachman?"

"I don't remember. They get a divorce. He move his things out two, three months ago and I never see him after that."

"When was your last contact with Mrs. Bachman?"

"I always call the night before I come, to check she still wants me. Sometimes she change the schedule. I call at nine o'clock last night."

"Was there anything unusual about your conversation? Did she sound upset in any way?"

"No. She just tell me come at eleven. She say she not be home. She had appointment. That's why I surprised when I find her in the bedroom."

"Did she say with whom she had an appointment?"

"Mrs. Bachman, she sell real estate. Maybe a client."

"I understand the door was locked when you arrived. Does anyone besides yourself and Mrs. Bachman have a house key?"

"No."

"What about Mr. Bachman?"

"Mrs. Bachman, she change locks after he move."

"Does she keep an extra key anywhere, in case she accidentally locks herself out?" Sanders asked.

"Yes. She hide it under plant pot on back patio. I don't know which pot."

"What about the alarm. Was it set when you arrived?"

"No. She always leaves alarm off when I come."

Daniel turned to Brenda. "Could you check the keypad at the entrance? See if the alarm is working, and call the alarm company to see when it was set and turned off last night."

"Sure."

"And see if you can locate the spare key," Sanders added.

Brenda left the kitchen and turned in the direction of the front door.

"Do you have any more questions for Mrs. Contreras?" Sanders asked Daniel. "She's had a very difficult day. I'd like to let her go home."

"I'm done for now. Thank you, Mrs. Contreras. If you could just leave your contact information with the Sergeant, in case one of us needs to talk to you again."

Daniel and Sanders left the kitchen and walked toward the entryway, where Brenda was beckoning them.

"Guys, the alarm is working fine. The security company said it was turned off at one o'clock this morning."

At that moment, the crime team and medical examiner arrived. Sergeant Sanders went upstairs to brief them. "If you two can wait a few minutes, the three of us can pay a visit to Phillip Bachman."

"I'll check the back patio while we're waiting," Brenda said.

She was back ten minutes later.

"I couldn't find a key anywhere," she said to Daniel. "You think the killer took the key, let himself in, turned off the alarm because he knew the code, and then killed her?"

"Sounds like something her husband could do, assuming she didn't think to change her code after she changed the locks. Or, she could have let him in."

"At one in the morning?"

"Let's see if the Sergeant can get a search warrant for Bachman's house and gym," Daniel said. "Maybe we'll all hit pay dirt."

CHAPTER FORTY-SIX

ALL AFTERNOON, I WAS EXPECTING Daniel to call me with news about Victoria Bachman, and I jumped every time the office phone rang. I wasn't a big fan of coincidence, and somehow, I was sure that Victoria's death and Louise's were connected.

When my receptionist said "Call for you, Dr. K," on the intercom, I picked up the receiver and said "Daniel?"

"Sorry to disappoint you. It's Frances."

"Hi, Frances. I'm happy to hear from you. What's up?"

"You are a very lucky woman. Last night, I decided I'd take the yearbook to bed and see if I could get through A-C. I found him in B. The boyfriend's name was Phillip Bachman."

I felt a chill run up my spine.

"Are you okay?"

"I'm fine," I said. "Phillip Bachman's estranged wife was my patient. He called me yesterday and threatened to sue me for wrongful birth if I delivered her."

"What did you say? Did you tell his wife?" Frances asked.

"I haven't seen her since. She died at home, sometime last night," I said. "The police are investigating. That's why I was expecting a call from Daniel."

Frances gasped. "Do you think Phillip could have killed Louise and his wife?"

"It's possible. Being Louise's ex-boyfriend certainly explains why he wanted his wife to change doctors, but not why he would have killed Louise."

"He couldn't have been carrying a grudge over a thirty-year-old failed romance, could he?" Frances said.

"Maybe. Some people carry grudges for a lifetime. I wonder if he knew Louise was on the board of Planned Parenthood? Daniel told me he saw videos of Phillip at FPA demonstrations. How did Louise wind up on the board, by the way? Did you recruit her when you became medical director?" I asked

"No, I didn't. She came to me and wanted to join. She was already in our President's Circle of donors and her medical expertise was a great asset to us. I remember her saying that Planned Parenthood was there for her when she needed them the most and she wanted to give back."

My heart started racing. "Did you ask her what she meant by that?"

"No. I didn't want to pry, but I've heard many of our patients say the same thing."

"Well, thanks for the food for thought," I said. "I think I'd better pass this nugget on to my beloved fiancé."

CHAPTER FORTY-SEVEN

D ANIEL, BRENDA AND SERGEANT Sanders drove over to
Basic-Fit Gym.

"I think only two of us should talk to Mr. Bachman," Sanders said. "Three cops breaking the news of your wife's death is a bit intimidating."

"You go," Brenda said to Daniel. "I'll mind the car."

The same smiling receptionist was at the front desk.

"Can I help you?"

"Beverly Hills Police," Saunders said. "We need to see Mr. Bachman."

"I'm sorry, he's not in today."

"Could he be at one of his other locations?" Daniel asked.

"I don't think so. He left me a message this morning saying he was taking the day off."

"Do us a favor," Sanders said. "Call the other gyms and see if he came in."

The receptionist made the calls, and shook her head.

"Does he have a land line at home?"

"No, just a cell."

"What's the number?" Daniel asked.

She wrote it down and handed him the slip of paper.

Daniel phoned.

The call went to voicemail.

"We'll stop by his home and see if he's there," Daniel said. He handed her his card. "Call me if he comes in. It's important."

"That was quick," Brenda said, as they returned to the car.

"Not there," Sanders said.

"Think he's on the run?" Daniel asked.

"Could be," Sanders said. "I'm going to call and see if we can get a search warrant for his house and office. He's certainly our number one suspect for his wife's murder."

"He's high on the list for Louise Waldman as well," Daniel said, as he read the text Hannah had just sent him. "He was Louise's ex-boyfriend."

"I'll call in a BOLO for his car," Brenda said.

Obtaining a warrant to search Bachman's home for evidence linking him to the murder of his wife and Louise Waldman was a tedious job, and occupied the remainder of the afternoon. Sanders had dispatched an unmarked car to keep an eye on Bachman's house. The patrol reported no sign of him.

It was dark by the time they received the warrant and located the landlord. Bachman's rental was owned by a Shimon Katz, who lived in a much grander home a few blocks north of Pico. He answered the door, visibly annoyed at having his dinner interrupted, but had no objection to handing over a house key to the property once he had perused the warrant.

Sanders phoned the patrol car and was informed that there was still no sign of Bachman. She asked them to wait there, to help with the search. Then, the three of them drove together to the house.

The home was dark, with no sign of indoor or outdoor lighting. They rang the doorbell, waited, then opened the door.

"Mr. Bachman," Sanders shouted. "Are you home? Beverly Hills Police."

They hadn't expected an answer and there was none. The five officers put on paper booties, coveralls and latex gloves, and entered the house, turning on lights as they went. With firearms in hand, they searched the house, noting the layout of the rooms.

"We're looking for evidence of a connection between Bachman and an organization called FPA, Fetal Protection Association," Daniel said. "We also suspect he may have held a woman hostage here and murdered her, so be alert for any sign of struggle, blood, duct tape or rope. Finally, we suspect he may have murdered his wife last night. Look for any paper or electronic communication between them."

"I'd like you two to search the living room, dining room and kitchen," Sanders said to the two patrolmen. "Detective Ross, would you mind starting in the master bedroom, Detective Jordan and I can tackle the study. When we're done, we can move to the garage."

The group went to work. The master bedroom contained an unmade king-sized bed, two bedside tables, and what appeared to be a kitchen chair. Daniel examined it without touching. There seemed to be traces of adhesive on the two front legs.

One night table was empty. The other had a clock radio and an ashtray, with several cigarette butts. There was an open box of condoms in the drawer, along with a tube of lubricant. A phone charger was plugged in at the side of the table, but there was no cell phone.

A closet with mirrored doors occupied one wall. It contained a dozen pair of new athletic shoes, and was sparsely populated with hoodies, sweat pants, and workout shorts. A handful of formal shirts, slacks, and sport jackets hung at the other end. Daniel worked his way through the pockets, found nothing.

There was no luggage in the closet, and most of the dresser drawers were empty of socks or underpants. One drawer contained a few faded T-shirts. Daniel removed all the drawers, and checked in the back and underneath. He examined the walls and floor, looking for a safe, but found none.

He proceeded into the bathroom. A dirty tub and plastic shower curtain showed signs of use. A damp towel hung over the towel rack. Daniel opened the medicine chest and found mouthwash, a bottle of Tums, and some aspirin. There were no prescription medications. He went through the few drawers under the sink, finding no toothbrush, toothpaste or shaver.

"Anything?" Brenda asked from the door.

"Yeah. We need a crime scene team. There's a chair in the bedroom that looks suspicious. Louise may have been tied to it. We need to check the garage for rope and duct tape."

Sanders joined them. "Where do you think he is?"

"He's gone," Daniel said. "I don't see any of the usual toiletries, and his underwear and socks are missing. The closet is mostly empty. No suitcases. You'd expect there to be some, if he'd recently moved in. You two find anything in the study?"

"Lots of boxes with files, but no computer. I think you're right. He packed his bags, took his electronics, and left," Sanders said.

"Hey, guys, have a look at this. We found it in the garbage can on the back porch."

One of the patrolmen was holding up a black plastic garbage bag. He reached in and handed Daniel a blue leather purse.

Daniel held it up by its strap. "Brenda, take a look inside."

Brenda put on a fresh pair of gloves, opened the purse, and extracted a wallet, a cell phone, two pens, a compact, a lipstick and a comb.

"The phone's dead," she said. "But I'll bet this is the burner we've been looking for." She put it back in the purse, along with the cosmetics. There were several twenty dollar bills in the wallet, but no credit card or driver's license. "If the purse belonged to Louise, either she didn't risk taking any ID to the FPA meeting, or Bachman removed and destroyed what was in here."

"Let's put it all in an evidence bag. Hopefully, it's got some useful prints, and some DNA," Daniel said.

Sergeant Sanders joined them in the bedroom. "I've got an evidence team on the way. I don't think there's much else for us to do here, other than check out the garage and wait for the forensics results."

"That, and trace Bachman," Daniel said.

CHAPTER FORTY-EIGHT

THE ENSUING FEW DAYS WERE AN agony of waiting: waiting for forensics, waiting for the massive effort to trace Phillip Bachman to uncover a lead. Daniel couldn't have been more frustrated.

"You know, pacing up and down the kitchen won't find him any faster," Hannah said.

Hannah was seated at the breakfast table nursing a large coffee, topped with foamy milk, and reading the Saturday Los Angeles Times. Daniel paused, reached for a mug, and poured himself some caffeine. He liked it black.

Hannah put down the paper and smiled at him, as he seated himself opposite her. She was wearing green plaid pajamas, and her long, red hair cascaded down her back. She looked relaxed and adorable.

"What are your plans for the day?" Daniel asked.

"I am going to put murder out of my mind and go wedding dress shopping with Andrea and Ruth."

Daniel grinned. "Don't let those two talk you into anything that will bankrupt us."

"Not to worry. I'll leave us enough money to pay for the honeymoon. Are you planning to work today?"

"I'm planning to work until we catch the bastard."

"Update me, please," Hannah said.

"We've got two police departments doing everything possible to track him. The forensics on the blue purse came back yesterday afternoon. It contained prints and DNA from both Bachman and Louise. We found duct tape in the garage, as well as rope, which match the trace evidence of adhesive and fibers found on her body, and on the chair in his bedroom.

"So, Phillip Bachman is definitely her killer."

"We have enough evidence to tie him to Louise's murder. It's a little more difficult to prove he killed Victoria. His prints and DNA are all over the house, but he lived there. They aren't on the keypad for the alarm, but he knew the code, and he also knew where she kept her spare key, even though she changed the locks. The spare key is still missing."

"So, he had motive, opportunity and enough knowledge to get into the house. What's being done to trace him?"

"We know he hasn't left the country, because his passport hasn't been used, and we've put an alert on it. If he tries to drive across the border, or get on an international flight, he'll be detained. We've checked the flight manifests for every national flight, from every airport within driving distance, and we've come up blank. We have a BOLO out for his car, but it hasn't been spotted yet."

"What do you think he's doing for money?" Hannah asked.

"The last thing we were able to trace was a large withdrawal from his business account, the day before Victoria died. It looks like he planned to kill her and then take off. He hasn't used his credit card or phone since then."

"Could he use Louise's credit cards, or Victoria's?"

"Louise's cards were cancelled by her husband, right after her death. Victoria's were in her wallet. If he wanted the police to assume the death was natural, he wouldn't steal anything from the house."

Hannah took a few more sips of her coffee and nibbled on a piece of buttered toast. "We know he liked to go backpacking. Could he be in the wilderness somewhere? Was there any camping equipment in his home?"

"Good question. There wasn't any, which suggests that he may have taken it with him. He was also the registered owner of a semi-automatic pistol and a rifle. Those were also missing from his home."

"So, you've got an armed fugitive, who knows his way around the wilderness, and could be anywhere."

"That sums it up," Daniel said. "The only hope is that there's a limit to how much food he can carry with him if he's camping. Even if he were an experienced hunter, it's pretty hard to live off the land. He's got to come to ground eventually. Izzy and a team are looking through all his paperwork and trying to find out if he, or his corporation, owns property, any place he might feel safe hiding out."

Hannah rose from her seat, rinsed her dishes, and massaged Daniel's shoulders. He leaned back, trying to relax without much success.

"If anyone can find him sweetheart, you and your team can."

"I hope you're right."

"I know I am. I'm going to get dressed now, and take Zoe to her play date," Hannah said. "I'll see you later."

He squeezed her hand. "Good luck on your wedding dress mission."

"Thanks," she said. "I suspect my hunt will be a little easier than yours."

CHAPTER FORTY-NINE

"Fɪʀsᴛ, ᴡᴇ ʜᴀᴠᴇ ʟᴜɴᴄʜ," Aɴᴅʀᴇᴀ announced. "A girl should never go shopping on an empty stomach."

"I second that," Ruth said.

Andrea drove us into Beverly Hills and pulled into the parking lot of the South Beverly Grill. I approved. They had a Thai steak salad that was to die for.

The three of us slid into a comfortable booth and ordered iced tea.

"Doesn't this feel just like Sex and the City?" Andrea said, after a satisfying sip of her drink. "We should do this more often."

"Carrie and her friends didn't have husbands and small children making demands on them. They could go to lunch whenever they wanted to, and spend their evenings drinking in trendy clubs," I said.

"Noisy trendy clubs with narcissistic guys," Ruth said. "I'd hate that."

The waiter brought my salad, a rare burger for Ruth, and a salmon mango roll for Andrea. We dug in.

"Hannah, what did you wear for your first wedding?" Andrea asked.

I thought back to my wedding to Ben, at the Harvard Club. It had been a joyful event with all our friends, and large numbers of aunts, uncles and cousins whom I hadn't seen since.

"It was a floor-length, strapless, white satin gown. No lace. No pearls. No glitz."

It had been gorgeous, and was sitting in a bag from the cleaners in a far corner of my closet. As I thought about it, I realized how long it had been since thoughts of Ben had crossed my mind. It had taken me five years to start thinking about dating, and even longer to overcome the feeling of betrayal I had struggled with, when Daniel and I finally became lovers. Thank goodness, he'd been so patient. I had absolutely no belief in an afterlife, but if there was one, I was sure Ben would have approved of my second marriage.

"So, what kind of a dress are we looking for this time?" Ruth asked.

"Something much less formal, and it doesn't have to be white."

"Don't forget, it needs to have room for expansion," Andrea said. "You could lose your waistline in the next six weeks."

"I hope so," I said.

We wound up going to Harari, my favorite boutique. I bought a pair of cream-colored, silk palazzo pants with elastic on the back of the waist, a matching camisole, and a floating silk cut velvet top with long sleeves. Those October evenings could be cool. Afterwards, we walked up to Nate and Al's Deli and shared a large piece of strawberry cheese-cake. "It's important to feed the baby," Andrea announced.

All in all, it was a perfect girls' afternoon, and murder did not once cross my mind.

CHAPTER FIFTY

IT WAS MONDAY BEFORE DANIEL HAD A break in the case, and as usual, it was Izzy who found the information.

"The guy owns a cabin," Izzy said. "His parents purchased it in the sixties, which is probably why I didn't find it online. It's near Johnsondale."

"Where the hell is that?" Daniel asked.

"It's the Southern Sierras, in Tulare County," Brenda said. "It's an area popular with hunters. My dad and brothers used to go there."

Daniel raised an eyebrow and reached for Izzy's copy of the deed.

"I brought it up on Google Earth," Izzy said.

Johnsondale was quite a bit south of Sequoia National Park. It looked like a very small town indeed. There were several dirt Forest Service roads in the vicinity, and the coordinates of Bachman's land appeared to be adjacent to one of them.

"He could have gone there. He might have supplies stored. Does the cabin have electrical or telephone service?" Daniel asked.

"No electricity. There's probably cell phone service but no landline. I doubt there's indoor plumbing or water, but the Kern River is close and there are probably creeks or springs he could use for water."

"Let's see if we can get in touch with local law enforcement. Maybe the Tulare County Sheriff can send a few guys to scope it out for us," Daniel said.

"It would be nice if they found Bachman's car, or even spotted him," Brenda said.

Daniel made the call. "The guy is wanted for two murders in Los Angeles. He's armed and dangerous."

"Don't you city boys worry," the sheriff said. "We know how to hunt out here. We'll let you know if we see him or find his car."

It was late afternoon when the sheriff called back.

"We've got your guy," he said. "What do you want us to do with him?"

"No kidding?" Daniel said. "I'm impressed."

"It was easy. We found his car, staked out the cabin, and waited for him to go to the outhouse to take a dump. Two deputies were outside with loaded guns when he came out."

"We are very grateful. Stick him in a cell, read him his rights, and we'll send a van to transport him to L.A. We'd also like to send up a crime scene team to search his cabin. Can you get a warrant?"

"You bet. See you in a few hours."

CHAPTER FIFTY-ONE

"I'M NOT GOING TO MAKE IT HOME FOR dinner tonight," Daniel told me. "I'll be back very late."

"What's going on?" I asked.

"Bachman's been captured. He's in a cell in Tulare County. We're going up there to question him, and to transfer him back to Los Angeles for arraignment."

I took a deep breath. I couldn't believe it was almost over.

"That's a relief. Daniel, I want to know why. Why did he kill Louise?"

"I want to know that as well," Daniel said. "And I also want to know how he knew where she would be that night."

"I'll try to wait up for you. If I fall asleep, you can tell me all about it in the morning."

CHAPTER FIFTY-TWO

Daniel and Brenda drove up to Johnsondale in a police car, followed by two more cops in a prisoner transfer van. Sergeant Sanders, and a Beverly Hills detective, drove separately. They all met at the County Jail, where a smiling sheriff shook their hands and regaled them, once again, with how his guys had stalked and hunted their suspect.

"Can we put him in an interview room for questioning?" Daniel asked.

"You got it," the sheriff said, and motioned to one of his deputies to move the prisoner.

Daniel turned to Sergeant Sanders. "Why don't Brenda and I begin questioning him about the Waldman murder? When we're done, you can ask him about his wife."

"Fine with us," Sanders said.

Phillip Bachman was seated in the interview room, his

hands in cuffs. He glared at Daniel and Brenda as they entered the room.

"Are you responsible for this? What the hell am I doing here?"

Daniel turned on a recording device and read Bachman his rights, offering him an attorney if he wished.

"I haven't done anything, and I don't need some piss-assed hick public defender," Bachman said. "What am I charged with?"

"You're being charged with the murder of Dr. Louise Waldman," Daniel said.

"I just sued her. I didn't murder her."

"That's not what the forensic evidence shows. We got a search warrant for your house. We found her purse, with her DNA and yours. The chair where you tied her with rope and duct tape, and tortured her. And the cigarette butts you used to burn her."

Bachman's lips tightened and his face began to turn an unhealthy shade of red. "You can't prove anything. Why would I kill her, when I could win a huge amount of money out of her for malpractice?"

"That's what we'd like to know," Daniel said. "We hear she was your college sweetheart. Is this revenge for a broken heart?"

"Broken heart, my ass. It's punishment for a bitch who committed murder."

Daniel knew when to keep quiet and when to ask more questions. Bachman's fury was building and an out-of-control, angry suspect was often a great source of information.

"She aborted my kid, without asking me or telling me. I only found out later. I would have married her, but she was much more interested in going to medical school than in marrying me. Abortion is murder. She's in hell, as we speak."

"You must have been shocked, when you went to West-side Fertility Associates and found out your wife's doctor was your former girlfriend," Daniel said.

"The hypocrisy of it," Bachman ranted. "There she was, passing herself off as a hot shot fertility specialist, helping other women to get pregnant, when she fucking didn't hesitate to kill my kid."

"I can see how you would feel that way," Daniel said. "I know how strongly you feel about abortion."

"Doctors who do abortions should be shot. Killing innocent babies."

"Are you a member of the Fetal Protection Association?"

Bachman shrugged. "I've gone to some of their demonstrations, but they mostly meet in Orange County. Too far to drive."

"I would think a guy who feels as passionately as you do on the subject would be in their inner circle."

"I didn't know they had an inner circle."

"How do you feel about Planned Parenthood?" Daniel asked.

"They should be shut down."

"Did you know that Louise Waldman was on their board of directors?"

"Yeah, I knew. I looked her up. The bitch was leading a double life, pretending to help women get pregnant with one hand, and doling out contraceptives and abortions with the other. She deserved what she got."

"Is that why you killed her, because she aborted your child, and you've had two wives with fertility problems?"

"I didn't intend to kill her. I wanted to beat the shit out of her. Things got out of control."

"How did you know where to find her?" Daniel asked.

"I followed her home, a few days after Vicki and I went to her office, so I knew where she lived."

"You must have been furious after you and your wife split up, and you found out that Louise had implanted embryos that should have been destroyed. I'm not surprised you sued her for malpractice. Did you stalk her when she left the office Thursday night?"

"I drove to her house and waited for her to come home. She left a few minutes later, in an old Honda, so I followed her. She parked in my neighborhood," Bachman said.

"So, you just waited for her to come back to her car and you kidnapped her?" Daniel said.

"Pretty much."

"What did you do then?"

"You've got the evidence. You know what I did. And I'd do it again."

Daniel leaned back in his chair. "Why don't we pause for now? We have a detective from the Beverly Hills Police Department with us, who wants to ask you a few questions about Victoria. We'll be transferring you back to Los Angeles as soon as they're finished with you."

"Whatever," Bachman said.

Daniel and Brenda left the room and motioned for Sergeant Sanders to go on in. Once the two of them reached the outer office, Daniel sought out the sheriff.

"We can't thank you enough for your help. Once the

Beverly Hills cops are done with their interview, we'll take him off your hands. Our transfer van is parked in your lot."

"No trouble," the sheriff said. "Glad we could help."

"We owe you one," Daniel said, then turned to Brenda. "How about we start heading home?"

CHAPTER FIFTY-THREE

I TRIED TO STAY AWAKE, WAITING FOR Daniel to get back, but sometime after 1:00 a.m., my eyelids closed, and the book I was reading slipped out of my hands. When I awoke at my usual time, Daniel was sound asleep beside me. I figured he was exhausted, so I quietly grabbed my clothes and dressed in the bathroom. I doubted he'd wake before I had to leave for the office, so I left him a warm pot of coffee, and a note with a smiley face and a few hearts.

I could wait until evening to hear the whole story.

Later that night, the two of us arrived home within minutes of one another, and hugged for a long time.

"It's over," Daniel said. "Bachman confessed."

"To both murders?" I asked.

"Just Louise so far. We might have trouble nailing him for Victoria's murder without a confession, but it doesn't matter. He'll spend the rest of his life in jail."

I drew Daniel into the living room and sat close to him on the sofa. I could see the fatigue on his face.

"You look wiped out," I said.

"I am. The paperwork took longer than the arrest."

"I'm so relieved. Did you find out why he did it?"

"Louise was his college girlfriend. She aborted his baby. I think seeing her as an infertility specialist ignited his rage."

"So that was what Louise meant, when she told Frances that Planned Parenthood had been there for her when she needed them the most. I suspected, but I wasn't sure."

"Have you ever had mixed feelings about performing abortions?" Daniel asked.

"No. My patients have mixed feelings. I've never met a woman who didn't struggle with her decision, but once that decision is made, my job is to help her. Every woman has the right to decide whether and when to have a baby."

"Speaking of babies," Daniel reached over and caressed my stomach. "Let's see if we can put the past few weeks behind us, and focus on all the happy things in our life."

I placed my hand over his and snuggled closer, resting my head on his shoulder.

"Great idea," I said. "Right now, nothing is more important than our wedding."

EPILOGUE

I WOKE AT 5:30 A.M. ON THE MORNING of our wedding, just as the sky was beginning to brighten. "Woke" is perhaps an exaggeration, as I don't remember getting much sleep. I was too agitated, and my mind refused to stop reviewing all the details. Daniel was sleeping like a baby beside me.

I slipped out of bed and tiptoed out of the room. I turned off the alarm system, opened the doors to the large deck that ran the length of our new house, and looked out over the canyon. It was the perfect place from which to view a sunrise, and to have the small, intimate wedding that we'd chosen.

The chairs for the ceremony, and the tables for the dinner afterwards, were already in place. The caterers would arrive later in the day with linens, tableware and all the fabulous food I'd ordered. I had also hired a photographer and a DJ, with a playlist of slow romantic songs, which hopefully wouldn't annoy the neighbors.

With a reassuring feeling that the key details were in place, I retreated to the living room.

"Mommy, why are you up so early?" Zoe was standing in

the entry, wearing Miss Kitty pajamas, and rubbing the sleep from her eyes.

"Why are *you* up so early?" I asked, giving her a hug.

"I'm the Maid of Honor. I have to be sure everything is ready."

"Would the Maid of Honor like some breakfast?"

"We should have chocolate chip pancakes," she announced. "Can I make them?"

I visualized the mess we were going to make in my immaculate kitchen and decided it was worth it. I set out all the ingredients on the table, with measuring cups and a big bowl, opened the cookbook to the pancake recipe, and told her to make the batter while I put up some coffee. Zoe was reading quite fluently, and I had no doubt she could navigate her way through the instructions.

I ground enough coffee beans for eight cups, poured in the water, and started the coffee maker. Then, I decided I should probably wake Daniel. He'd never forgive me if he missed out on chocolate chip pancakes.

Daniel opened his eyes to find Hannah standing beside the bed. She was still wearing her high-necked, long-sleeved, white cotton nightgown. Her curly red hair cascaded, uncombed, down her back.

"Good morning, sleepyhead," she said.

Daniel reached out and pulled her on top of him, so he could kiss her. It was the perfect way to start the morning.

"We should probably save this for our wedding night," she said, rolling over beside him. "If we do it now, we'll miss out on Zoe's chocolate chip pancakes."

Daniel laughed. "I guess I'd better get up and brush my teeth then. I wouldn't want to keep Zoe waiting."

Hannah joined him at the other sink, splashing cold water on her face and running a brush through her hair. Every time he looked at her he marveled at the fact that this beautiful, smart, sexy woman was about to marry him.

"Nervous?"

"A little, but I'm pretty sure I'm marrying the right guy."

"That's a relief," he said.

He slipped behind her and pulled her into an embrace. Giving her a final kiss on the back of the neck, he took her hand and they headed for the kitchen.

Chocolate chip pancakes turned out to be the perfect choice for breakfast. Whenever I've felt an anxiety attack coming on, I've always turned to chocolate, or ice cream, or chocolate ice cream. All of those were far more effective than Valium.

After breakfast, Daniel and Zoe announced that they were doing the dishes, and they shooed me out of the kitchen with the L.A. Times.

I took the paper to our bedroom, settled into my reading chair, and tried to focus. There wasn't much new in the news, and none of it was cheerful. There wasn't anything, except perhaps Doonesbury, that I wanted to read on my wedding day.

I discarded the paper, walked to my closet, and took my outfit out of its plastic cover. It looked pretty good, even if I never got to wear it again. Daniel had given me a pair of antique emerald and diamond earrings to go with my engagement ring, and just for fun, I'd purchased emerald green high heels to match.

The reception was all organized, and I was going to look acceptable in the wedding pictures, so why was my stomach fluttering, as if I was about to take the medical boards again? I loved Daniel. He loved me, and had certainly proved himself over the past two years, during any number of stressful situations, but what if this was all a horrible mistake? I'd been so happy with Ben. What if this second marriage just didn't measure up?

I walked over to my desk and opened the bottom drawer, to which I had consigned Ben's photo in its silver frame. It hadn't seemed appropriate to display it in the bedroom, once Daniel moved in. I stared at Ben's face, with the high cheekbones, prominent nose and curly, dark hair.

"So, Ben, what do you think?" I asked.

"I think you should put me back in the drawer, and hide that outfit before Daniel sees it. Then, you should go have some ice cream."

I frequently had mental conversations with my former spouse. His advice was usually sound. I put the outfit back in the closet, and went to check the freezer. Perhaps we had some Belgian Chocolate Häagen Dazs stashed away.

I had scheduled the ceremony for five in the afternoon, at which time the deck would be in the shade. There wasn't much of an aisle between the glass doors that led from the dining room outside, but we each walked it slowly, to the accompaniment of music.

Andrea was first, positioning herself to face the guests. Then came Daniel, resplendent in a tailored navy blue suit, and his parents. Zoe followed, in a royal blue dress. Zoe hates wearing dresses, but made an exception for the wedding.

Finally, it was my turn, accompanied by my parents. Daniel stepped forward, took my hand, and gave me a look of total adoration.

Andrea cleared her throat and began her speech. I was having trouble focusing on what she was saying, but I did catch the word "vows."

Daniel reached into his breast pocket and removed a sheet of paper.

"Hannah, I'm still in awe that I'm standing here today, marrying the most extraordinary woman I've ever known. I've seen the care and compassion you devote to your patients, your dedication as a mother, your keen intelligence and determination, as you try to solve the most demanding puzzles, and the warmth, love and loyalty you give to me, and to your friends and family. I feel honored to be your husband and promise that I will always be there for you, no matter what happens in our lives together. "

Daniel squeezed my hands, and there were tears in both our eyes.

I, of course, didn't have any pockets in my wedding dress, but it didn't matter. I'd memorized my vows.

"Daniel, when I met you, I was in pain. You appeared in my life as a kind of miracle. Your love has sustained and supported me. Your new adventure, becoming Zoe's father, has been a joy for me to watch. I have always been confident that I could count on you. I want nothing more than to spend my life with you, as my husband. "

"I believe it is now time for me to pronounce you married, and for you to kiss," Andrea said, with a grin.

Daniel and I slid our arms around one another and

complied. It was a very long kiss, and accompanied by much applause.

We stared into one another's eyes for a moment, before we turned to face our family and friends. Zoe ran over to us, and we each took her by the hand. She looked up, beaming. Daniel and I smiled at her and at one another. The ceremony was over. It was time for our new life, as a family, to begin.

ACKNOWLEDGMENTS

First and foremost, I'd like to thank my editor and writing teacher, Linda Schreyer, whose editorial skills have made all of my books so much better, and my publisher Christiana Miller for her confidence in my books. My thanks as well to my fellow writing student, Cathy Novak, for all her encouragement and insightful feedback, and for the support I've always gotten from my writing retreat group, Darlene, Hyla, Laurie and Erica.

Special thanks to Drs. Rebecca Sokol and Hal Danzer for several fascinating conversations about ethical issues in infertility. Defense attorney Jerry Bernstein made certain I didn't embarrass myself in the scenes involving lawyers and the FBI. Prize-winning reporter, Darcy Spears, educated me on hidden cameras. Suzy Lamson, poet and Punctuation Queen copyedited the first edition of the manuscript. My husband, Uri, is always my first reader and IT expert. Thank you all. I couldn't have written this without you.

ABOUT THE AUTHOR

Paula Bernstein is a New York native, who migrated to LA to attend graduate school in Chemistry. She acquired a PhD, an exceptionally nice husband, and the ability to synthesize creative meals from leftovers. Not long afterwards, she escaped her laboratory and attended medical school.

Like her series heroine, Hannah Kline, Paula spent her professional life practicing Obstetrics and Gynecology. When she developed an irresistible desire for an uninterrupted nights' sleep, she retired from her full time practice, and reinvented herself as a writer of medical mysteries.

Learn more about her at her website: https://www.hannahklinemysteries.com/

ALSO BY PAULA BERNSTEIN

The Hannah Kline Mysteries

Murder in the Family

Murder by Lethal Injection

Murder in a Private School

Murder in the Goldilocks Zone

Murder in Vitro

Murder on Her Honeymoon

Murder is a Nightmare

Murder is a Hate Crime

Murder is Paralyzing

Short Stories

Potpourri

www.ingramcontent.com/pod-product-compliance
Lightning Source LLC
Chambersburg PA
CBHW021429150726
47989CB00001B/176